OSPREY REEF

OSPREY REEF
VICTORIA McKERNAN

Carroll & Graf Publishers, Inc.
New York

Thanks to Peter Boundy, who knew how much I wanted
to dive

First Carroll & Graf edition 1990

Carroll & Graf Publishers, Inc
260 Fifth Avenue
New York, NY 10001

Library of Congress Cataloging-in-Publication Data

McKernan, Victoria.
  Osprey Reef / Victoria McKernan. — 1st Carroll & Graf ed.
    p.   cm.
  ISBN: 0-88184-635-X : $17.95
  I. Title.
 PS3563.C3756087   1990
 813'.54—dc20   90-43429
                                                    CIP

Manufactured in the United States of America

To my father, John Vincent McKernan, who let us climb on the rocks even out to the edge.

OSPREY REEF

Chapter 1

"Hola! Hola! Wait, yourself. I'm untied all over the place!" Umbi panted as he ran down the dock, one sneaker flapping. He dropped his bag and set his lanky form down next to it. "Dis way too early for morning, my friend." Chicago pulled the bag into the skiff and stowed it in the crate with the rest of the scuba gear.

"It's sunrise, amigo. What's the matter, you got a soft bed and the comfortable life somewhere?"

"Sunrise! What fish gonna care about is it sunrise? Dey just swimming around. Dey don't get out'a no bed and take no shower and make no coffee, dey have no dog to walk around the block!"

Chicago laughed at his energetic protests and started one outboard. Umbi tossed his sneakers into the boat and untied the lines, pushing them away from the dock with one foot as he climbed aboard.

"You got both of 'em running again?" he said admiringly as Chicago adjusted the choke on the second motor.

"I hope so, I put in new fuel lines and cleaned the carburetor. There was crap around the plugs, too."

She expertly twisted the two throttles until the engines settled into a healthy unison roar, and they sped out into the bay. The sun wasn't up yet, but a flat band of dull yellow lay on the horizon beneath a cloudless sky. Miami was at its quietest at this time of the day, and for a few minutes Chicago almost liked it. The ocean was calm, the wind faint. With any luck they could make the reef in half an hour, collect some fish in maybe another two or three hours, and be back by ten or eleven. She didn't have to be at the marina until noon but hoped to be able to look at Sanford's valve cover gasket before that.

"Where we going and what we catchin' today?" Umbi asked as he rummaged through the dry-bag and pulled out one of the sandwiches she had brought.

"Piranha," she replied. "You're bait."

"Yah—good, they nibble off me toes and I don't have no trouble wid the shoes fit no more," Umbi replied insolently.

Chicago laughed. After two years in America, Umbi had mastered English and could as easily put on the accent of a Harvard professor as use his native patois. This early in the morning, however, his tongue usually lapsed into the slack edges of Caribbean speech.

"So where we goin'?"

"Osprey Reef. It's there on the chart," Chicago replied, handing him the plastic chart bag. "Seventy-nine-degrees forty longitude and about twenty-six-thirty five latitude."

"Nobody go there," Umbi mused, studying the page sideways, on purpose. Chicago had been trying to teach him some navigation but was getting nowhere. Umbi was a quick learner when he wanted to be and impossibly stubborn the rest of the time.

"I know dis map stuff vital to you, but I just go where I going," he insisted. And she had to admit, once he went to a spot, he could always find it again. "I smell for it," he explained. "I recognize the waves."

He folded the chart up and tucked it away, smiling at Chicago's disapproving glance. Umbi was sixteen, tall and skinny, with man-size feet and broad hands. Although he had started to fill out recently and looked less scrawny, his limbs still seemed long and loose-jointed. Umbi was Haitian, with a mix of Spanish, African, and Creole blood that left him with light green eyes, high cheekbones, and skin the color of mink.

Despite their friendship, Chicago knew little about his family and past. She knew he had come to Miami in a small boat, along with hundreds of others, right before the fall of Baby Doc. She knew his father had been a fisherman and his mother a teacher in their rural village. He sometimes talked about fishing with his brothers but never said much about his homeland. He mentioned his father once, and somehow Chicago had the idea that he was in jail, but she did not press him for details.

She had found him sleeping in a shed behind the gas pumps one morning about a year ago, hungry and homeless but proud and a little bossy even then. He pronounced the shed an affront to waterfront aesthetics (actually, "broke-down slum-doghouse" was closer to his exact words) and offered to paint it for an exorbitant fee. After considerable negotiation, a lower price was agreed upon and the job was done well.

Chicago had started giving him odd jobs around the marina. Umbi had quickly proven himself smart and capable and eventually won the trust of others. Now he was called on by boat owners for all sorts of odd jobs, and Chicago was teaching him small-engine repair. He had taken up residence with Alfred, the night watchman, a widower who lived in a little frame house a half mile down the road.

"So how come we going to Osprey?" Umbi asked.

" 'Cause no one goes!" Chicago replied with some triumph. "It's not good for sport diving because it was a missle-test site for years and that wrecked all the coral. It's a weird place as I remember; Dad charted part of it once. Once there were two small atolls. They just barely broke the surface. It made it dangerous to navigate around. Then the air force bombed the tops off them for target practice."

Umbi finished his sandwich and took the wheel. Chicago scanned the horizon with binoculars, looking for the color changes that would indicate the reef.

"Osprey is a long curving reef with a deep trench to the seaward side," she said. "There's a wide ledge at about fifty feet, then these two atolls sticking out."

"So what's so special about it for fish collecting?"

"I figure it's been twenty years since they were blasting there. The coral has probably started regenerating, and it could be a good place for expensive little fish. The Baltimore aquarium wants a school of lookdowns, and they like trenches. A net full of those babies will bring in four to five hundred dollars."

"What else?" Umbi asked as he started to arrange the nets and collection gear for the dive.

"Spotted eagle rays are going for up to four hundred fifty, and Boston's offering three hundred dollars for a five-foot nurse shark. There's some deep-water fish in demand, but I don't think Osprey's a good place for that."

"How come? I don't mind going deep."

"It's the fish that mind coming up," she said as she pulled the throttle back, nearing their destination. "Deep-water fish have to be decompressed over a couple of days or they die. Osprey's too far out to bother with that. Unless we find a good moray, too," she added. "Disney World has been looking for one."

"How we gonna catch a moray?" Umbi asked. He had only begun to accompany her on collection dives, and his previous fishing experience was for food. It didn't matter what condition the specimen was in then.

"Last time I got a moray, I spent a couple of weeks hand feeding him until he would come out of his hole, then netted him on the way back in."

"Oooh, maybe I better give you back this," he joked, holding out the last piece of his second sandwich. "Eating out your hand sounds dangerous."

They dropped the anchor on a patch of sand in thirty feet of water near the edge of Osprey Reef and quickly set up their scuba gear. Umbi had his own mask, snorkel, and fins, and Chicago loaned him the rest of the gear from the dive shop. He made a face as she handed him the B.C.

"C'mon, toad brain, you know you have to wear it." In Haiti, Umbi had learned to dive with a minimum of equipment, and he didn't like the buoyancy compensator, or B.C. She had had to train him out of more than a few bad habits.

"I won't tell nobody." He grinned hopefully.

She threw it into his lap. "First of all, I don't want to have to look at your skinny ol' bare-boned body, and second . . ."

"Yeah, yeah—as a PADI instructor you must always use all this shit."

Umbi slipped the backpack part of the B.C. over the tank and flipped the tension band over to hold it snug.

"I know you think it's geeky," Chicago continued as she screwed her regulator on her tank. "I didn't learn with one and I didn't like wearing it at first either, but someday I promise you'll be glad you have it."

The B.C.s were old-model jackets in faded orange. Newer B.C.s came with an endless array of gadgets and pockets and special features, in colors that would blind Peter Max. They were all essentially the same, however: an inflatable vest, with a hose that connected to the first stage of the regulator. A diver could push one button and inflate the vest with air from the tank to float on the surface, push another and let the air out to sink. Underwater, small regulations in the amount of air in the B.C. allowed a diver to adjust to whatever the water pressure was at a certain depth, thereby staying neutrally buoyant.

* * *

Chicago pulled on the bottom farmer-johns half of her wet suit and tossed the jacket to Umbi. If they stayed above sixty feet for this dive, they could spend an hour catching fish and even seventy-degree water would feel a little chilly. Once they had their gear on, Umbi rolled backward into the water and Chicago handed him the nets, then she slid in.

Chicago noted the time, then gave a nod and a thumbs-down sign and they slipped beneath the surface. Chicago had been diving most of her life but still got a thrill from the initial descent. It was like flying. Underwater, everything felt right. Although her father claimed she couldn't remember because she had been only three or four, she did remember the first time she saw this world.

He had returned to Trinidad from a long voyage and brought her a tiny mask. She remembered the strange smell of the rubber and the heavy feel of it against her face as he tightened the straps. He took her in his arms and waded out in the lagoon. She put her face in the water for a few seconds, then pulled it back out again and screamed. She remembered seeing her mother through the drops on the mask, reaching for her, thinking she was frightened. But it was thrill, not terror, she felt, and afraid her mother would take her out of the water, Chicago, regardless of air, had pushed out of her father's arms, launching herself into the world she had just glimpsed.

She glided down now, turning lazily to watch her bubbles floating like music toward the sky. Umbi held the net between his knees and, with his arms out like a bird, spiraled down, turning somersaults with the weightless freedom. Once on the bottom, Chicago checked the anchor, startling a little peacock flounder out of the sand. It swam gracefully past her, its soft blue-spotted "wings" undulating, and settled down again with a little swirl of sand. She signaled an okay to Umbi, and together they swam over to the edge of the reef.

Here the reef sloped gradually for about twenty feet, then fell away abruptly into a vertical wall. The water was clear in the shallower depth but stirred-up and cloudy in the trench below.

All around lay lumps of broken and dead coral long overgrown with algae. New coral, sponges, and plants had indeed started to grow again after the missile testing had stopped, but the reef still looked barren. It was an eerie place.

Umbi glanced at Chicago. She saw uneasiness in his eyes and, pulling out her regulator, made a face at him. Umbi laughed and water leaked into his mask.

They slipped down the face of the reef wall side by side, searching among the plants and rocks for the sought-after fish. There was a handsome scrawled filefish, worth $50, and a large, show-quality queen angelfish, also worth $50. A half-dozen barracuda sliced their silvery way past. What did they go for these days and which aquarium might want some? Naw. She decided they would be too hard to catch and transport. It did detract somewhat from the aesthetic part of diving to see each bright specimen with a price tag on its fin, but it was a living; well—part of it, anyway.

Umbi looked under rocks and into holes. He was good at finding the porcupine fish that were often hiding here. They were odd-looking fish that when frightened puffed themselves up into a spiny balloon. Despite their ferocious appearance, they were docile and could be handled gently with gloves.

In one of the holes he saw a long green face, two glittering eyes, and a mouthful of sharp teeth—a nice moray eel. Umbi rapped on his tank and Chicago swam over to see. She nodded in appreciation. Judging from the size of the eel's head, the rest of him could be five or six feet long. Maybe it would be worth cultivating a friendship with the beast. Osprey Reef was starting to look like a gold mine.

There were lots of small fish around, butterfly fishes and hamlets, yellow and blue tangs, but Chicago didn't collect them. They were plentiful and pretty but almost worthless. They could be had by the barrelful from the Dominican Republic. With the rising popularity of home marine aquariums, there was a high demand for fish and too many people were willing to ignore the harmful practices some collectors practiced. Most stores didn't care that the fish were being collected by poisoning the reef with arsenic or Clorox, to stun the fish. No matter that it killed twice as many fish as were collected.

Chicago had a good reputation and collected exclusively for aquariums, so she did all right. She still had mixed emotions about it, but a few pricey specimens would help if she was ever going to get the money to refit her boat. Just then, she spied the silver school she had been hoping for: a dozen or more lookdowns swimming slowly in formation along the top of the trench. The fish were odd-looking—square-shaped and narrow, bright silver, as if they had just been polished. With eyes set low over their jaws, they did indeed seem to be looking down all the time.

Chicago signaled to Umbi. Time to lay their trap. The net was six feet by twenty, made of clear, fine mesh, weighted on the bottom, and supported by flexible plastic strips every few feet. Along the top Chicago had attached small inflatable bags to hold it up. Once positioned in a good spot, they would swim a loop and herd fish into it. When trapped, fish tended to swim back and forth, not up and down, so they would have a little time to bring the ends in, corral the fish, and choose the ones they wanted.

They secured the nets, swam back along the reef, and circled behind the school. So intent was Chicago on collecting her bounty that she didn't notice the sharks. Umbi was also distracted, trying to watch Chicago's movements and learn how this was done. Slowly, like sheep dogs, they chased the fish up against the reef wall and let them swim in the direction of the net. As soon as the fish hit the mesh, Chicago grabbed one end and swam it around them while Umbi dove down and gathered up the bottom.

Umbi didn't look when he felt a bump against his collection bucket, thinking it had just bounced against a rock. He was trying to hold the net together as the frantic prisoners thrashed in panic inside. Each fish was about the size of a plate, so their combined struggle made for a lot of thrashing. When he felt a second bump, he glanced down. A burst of bubbles escaped as he gasped. Two lookdowns escaped as he lost his grip on the net.

Umbi felt a sharp taste of fear in the back of his throat and the stinging scrape of the broken coral against his legs as he backed against the reef. They were surrounded by sharks. At least a dozen were circling close by, and more shadowy forms appeared in the depths below.

Umbi grabbed at Chicago. She turned, puzzled, saw the panic in his eyes, then saw beyond him to their sudden company. In the endlessly long seconds that followed, Chicago thought a dozen different things: Where did they come from? Why are they threatening us? How will I pay off the new mast if I don't catch some fish today? What in hell do we do now?

She turned to Umbi, still holding the net with one hand. She squeezed his arm and pushed him against the reef, then turned her palms toward him in a signal to wait. Just don't panic, she willed silently.

Chicago had seen lots of sharks but never so many behaving so aggressively. They swam with backs arched, fins pointed down, in sharp, darting motions. They were mostly reef sharks, three- to-six-foot-long blacktips, but she spotted a few lemons, and some in the shadows had the fatter blunt shape of bulls. She knew that the sharks were a much greater threat if they thrashed around the sharks, but was it also true that they could sense the tiniest electrical twitching within a nervous muscle? Absurdly, she could see the whole two-page story from *Science Today,* complete with three-color graphs depicting this amazing and recently discovered ability. Great.

She took a deep breath and tried to calm the pounding in her ears. Umbi was breathing rapidly and seemed paralyzed. Suddenly, a shark darted close and bumped her collection bucket. Chicago unclipped it and let it fall. Another shark hit it, bumped once, attacked, and the two ripped it to shreds. Another absurd thought stuck in her brain, fear that eating the plastic would harm the shark. Umbi quickly unclipped his bucket and practically pitched it to the mob. Good, Chicago thought, he's thinking. The hell with eating plastic! With a huge tug, the collection net was ripped from her grip and the sharks set upon the trapped fish. It had cost over $200 in materials to make and contained hundreds of dollars' worth of prize specimens, but it was clearly destined for the buffet today.

Chicago let it go. She turned to Umbi and gave him the okay. She wondered if her eyes looked as scared as his, but she didn't know how to change them if they did. Motioning him to follow suit, she unclipped the buckles of her B.C. Keeping her regulator in her mouth, she slowly pulled the straps off and swung the scuba tank around in front. Umbi nodded and did the same. With their backs against the reef and the tanks held like battering rams in front of them, Chicago and Umbi felt more secure.

Now what? Wait it out? Swim away? Umbi nudged her arm and pointed urgently to the surface. He was breathing fast. Chicago nodded again and signaled—palms out, then one thumb pointing up, then thumb and forefinger pinched close: Slow, go up, little bit. Umbi nodded.

Slowly, without kicking, they let themselves drift up a few feet. The sharks continued to tear at the net and made no advances. Inch by inch, backs to the reef wall, tanks in front for protection, they began to creep upward. Suddenly, they heard the whine of a motor overhead. Umbi almost leapt toward the surface, and Chicago had to grab him. There were rules of diving to consider, too, and too rapid an ascent was just as deadly as being ripped apart by sharks. More urgently, she repeated the signal for SLOW. A boat was approaching. They heard it slow down, then idle. Gazing at the surface, looking for rescue, wondering what another boat was doing way out here, they took their eyes off the sharks.

Chicago's depth gauge swung up, then drifted back down against her leg. Perhaps it was the sudden movement, perhaps the bright yellow plastic, but one shark found it an attractive morsel.

The bite was more pressure than pain. She thought for a second that a rock had fallen on her leg. Then she felt her scuba unit being yanked away, the gauge clamped in the teeth of a blacktip shark with a scar on its head the shape of Alaska. Her regulator was torn from her mouth, bruising her teeth. The unbuckled B.C. jacket slipped off her arms. She grabbed at the hose but missed. It fell away.

Umbi hadn't seen the strike, but he felt her body jolt downward, saw the tank straps slipping off Chicago's arms, and dove down after it. He caught a corner of the B.C. almost losing his own gear in the process. Handling the two units was awkward. Umbi slipped one arm back through his own vest and tugged on Chicago's. Her dangling regulator got snagged on some coral and the hose was wedged tight. He felt Chicago by his side, turned, and saw her signaling for air. Thinking fast, Umbi pulled his own regulator out and handed it to Chicago. She took two quick breaths, then handed it back, dropped down, and untangled her regulator while Umbi balanced the tank.

In another couple of minutes they had recovered themselves and retreated again to the reef wall to get their equipment back on. Chicago felt dazed. Her depth gauge was gone, and a stream of bubbles poured from the ripped hose. Between that and their rapid breathing, the tanks were almost dry. She glanced at the surface, scanning for the hull of their anchored boat. It would be best to come up right under it. The sharks, strangely enough, had calmed down, even retreated somewhat. They continued their slow survey but did not approach again. They simply glided around, expressionless eyes on the terrified pair.

The color red disappears ten feet below the surface. When Umbi saw the black cloud flowing from the leg of Chicago's wet suit it took him a few seconds to register what it was: blood. He had not realized she had been bitten. Now he did not stop to consider the merits of slow, steady action. He thought only of the solid bottom of the boat and how good it would feel to have it between them and the sharks. He grabbed Chicago's hair and, pulling hard, bolted to the top.

They hit the surface, bursting into the blazing morning. It was a shock, like landing on another planet. It seemed the ascent had taken ten minutes and the thirty feet had been three miles. The surface of the water was like silk. The sun pounded. Chicago felt stunned, disconnected. Everything seemed surreal and exaggerated. She heard a buzzing in her ears, felt a strange and overwhelming sense of tranquility.

Umbi had let go of her and was a few feet away, treading water too fast, turning frantically and looking for something, shouting something she couldn't understand. Chicago pulled her mask down around her neck and rubbed the salty sting from her eyes, took a deep breath and tried to make sense of the moment. Then a shudder of fear swept through her, hitting like a block in the chest and rippling outward with a burn. The sharks.

Fighting the fear, she pulled her mask back on and peered below. She could see the sharks circling below, but they appeared to be retreating to the canyon. She saw the jagged tear in her wet suit and the little stream of blood still flowing out of it. Wincing with pain, she pulled the unripped section of neoprene up to cover the wound.

Chicago raised her head again. Umbi was struggling to stay afloat. "Umbi, hey, Humberto," she whispered, wondering why she was whispering. "Inflate your B.C." He had fallen suddenly quiet and didn't respond, just looked at her, his expression flat. She recognized the signs of silent panic. "C'mere. You'll float better." She paddled close and pushed his auto-inflator. The air rushed into the vest and he floated higher in the water. "It's okay, they're gone." Umbi didn't respond. She held tight to his shoulder strap and looked around, only now realizing what he had been screaming about.

Their skiff was gone, drifting some hundred yards away in the current. The buzzing in her ears was from another boat, now only a speck in the distance, speeding away.

Chapter 2

Alex Sanders leaned on the wooden rail at the stern of the boat and lifted his face for a breath of air. His palms were cold and clammy and his hands shook a little. He tried to shift his weight back to his rubbery legs but then felt another swell in his stomach and was forced to lean out over the gunwales again.

"Ahhh, it's a seafarin' life for me, lad!" shouted Wonton merrily as he shifted to neutral, allowing his friend to heave easier. "Nothing like it, eh! The salt air, the freedom of the sea!" He lifted the lid of the cooler and searched for the last bottle of orange crush. "And don't forget the rich bounty of her hidden depths!" He laughed as he held up the one small barracuda that made up their entire morning's catch.

Alex groaned and slumped onto a pile of coiled rope in the stern, accepted the bottle of soda, and took a sip, grimacing at the sweetness. "This stuff is lurid."

"Make a man out of you," Wonton insisted, beating his burly chest. Wonton (Frank) Baxter was a big man. He stood six feet four and weighed in at slightly less than a prize bull. The softening that had started with turning forty had smoothed over the muscle a little, left a little extra padding around the vulnerable middle, but did nothing to diminish the impression of sheer mass.

The original nickname One Ton had been corrupted sometime

during his early days on the police force. No one remembered exactly how it had started. Some said it was from the sixteen stitches and the resulting scar over Wonton's left eye, which left it looking slightly Oriental, some said it was because he was as big as a sumo wrestler.

"So how you feeling now, Sinbad?"

Alex shook his head and swallowed to clear the bitter taste. "Like I was kicked in the stomach—and have the flu . . . after eating rotten fish . . . while hung over from a long drunk on cheap wine."

"Ah, an experience I can't say I can relate to."

"I thought you said it wouldn't be rough." Alex groaned as he pulled himself up. He stumbled forward and grabbed the back of the captain's chair as Wonton pushed the throttle forward and spun them back to course. Wonton's boat was a clunky old fishing vessel, having survived so long on luck and attitude and several unorthodox engine repairs. It was twenty feet long and beamy. It rocked and bobbed in the flattest seas like a toy duck in a Jacuzzi.

"Rough!" Wonton shouted over the noise of the engine. "This, my landlocked mate, is almost flat calm!"

Alex wiped the cold sweat from his forehead and took another deep breath. He gazed out over the water and had to agree; it did look pretty calm.

"Listen, Wonton, it really was nice of you to take me out fishing and I've had a lot of fun, but next time I think I'll just stay home and stick needles in my eyes." He hadn't even thought about seasickness this morning, it had been so long since he was on a boat.

Growing up in Pierce County, North Dakota, the only hint of the ocean Alex had was the amber waves of grain. As a boy he had dreamed of the sea. He read sailing adventures and dreamed about running away and joining the merchant marine or building a boat to sail around the world. But he had never even seen an ocean until he was eighteen, when he flew over one on his way to Vietnam. Seasick! How ignoble. Well, he had gotten over it before; he probably just needed to get used to it again.

Alex turned his gaze inland, searching for the comforting sight of the Miami shoreline. As his gaze skimmed the horizon, something caught his eye, something shiny, a flash of color.

"Hey, Wonton!" Wonton couldn't hear him over the motor, and Alex stepped back to the helm and shouted in his ear. "Look out there—over there." He pointed. Wonton handed him a pair of binoculars, and Alex bent them in to fit his own eyes, focused, and scanned the horizon again, fighting another wave of nausea from the magnified vision.

"People!" he shouted, grabbing Wonton's arm and handing him the glasses. "In the water!" Wonton slowed the boat and looked for himself. "Christ!" he muttered, and scanned to both sides of the figures. "No boat, nothing—how'd they get there?" He dropped the binoculars, spun the wheel, and pushed the throttle full forward.

They were late for the squad meeting. Captain Torrance looked up expressionlessly as they entered, but his displeasure was palpable.

"Sorry, Captain." Wonton, never one to be meek, grinned the careless apology as he strode into the room and pulled out his chair. "Caught ourselves a mermaid! Took a while to reel her in. Did we miss anything?"

The meeting was routine—updates on investigations, details of an upcoming stakeout. A small but steady supply of cocaine was coming in through a fish market every week, and they were planning an undercover bust for the following Friday. Caron Morales, a small-time but elusive dealer, was involved, and it might just be their chance to finally nail him.

Alex felt his mind wandering. Just going through the motions, he thought. The emptiness, the flat worn-outness that had plagued him for the past year, had lifted a little that morning but was now settling back in like a great dusty hen.

Even with the seasickness, it had been a good morning. He liked Wonton. They had only been partners for six months, but there was a good rapport, a mutual respect, and a certain irreverence toward authority that they shared. God, how he missed having friends. It was a good time, an honest time: full of diesel smell and bait. Oh, come on—you're longing for a fucking beer commercial, he chastised himself. His business had never left much room for male bonding.

Alex sat up straight and tried to look interested in the meeting. He knew what subtle things to do with his posture and expression to achieve whatever look he wanted. That ability, as much as his features, had enabled him to pass in a variety of covers for years.

He had an angular face, with deep-set brown eyes, a strong jaw, and slightly prominent cheekbones that gave a hint of his grandmother's Slavic heritage. Until the gray strands had started appearing after the bad stint in Colombia, his hair had been dark brown, almost black, and something of an embarrassment to him. It was a thick head of fine, glossy hair, with a 1940s movie idol wave to it. Old ladies, blond bimbos, and fashionable men loved it; even an elephant in the zoo had once reached out to touch it, leaving a smelly thread of trunk goo on his forehead. The kind of woman Alex favored usually mistrusted it. "A little too *GQ,*" one had informed him. He liked to keep it either short enough to thwart the waviness or long enough for a ponytail. It could use a trim now, he thought absently, although it was hard to find anyone in Miami who wasn't a damn *stylist.*

Captain Torrance was briefing them on a continuing investigation, the murder of a local real estate developer/money launderer.

He had been found in his car, shot through the head in a typical drugland execution style.

". . . so forensics reports give us nothing special—no witnesses. We're questioning his lawyer . . ." he droned on.

Alex was restless; he let his mind wander. This rescue business —too unbelievable. Beautiful damsel rescued from man-eating sharks. Actually, he wasn't sure if she was beautiful or not, having only seen her dripping wet and dressed in neoprene. They had radioed for an ambulance to meet them at the dock, and Alex couldn't think of any excuse to follow them to the hospital.

The event had brought back that certain thrill. He shook his head and sat up straight, stretched in his chair, and tried to concentrate on the meeting. I'm not looking for thrills anymore, he reminded himself. He had taken the Miami job hoping it might be a good initiation to real life. Whatever that was.

He looked around the table, his glance lingering on Dell Peterson and Jack Roscoe for a second, the scum. He skipped over Barnes and Hollings, and his gaze lingered on Torrance. Now, there was a complicated man. The captain was fifty-four, married for thirty-one years, with three grown children, a modest lifestyle, an undistinguished but satisfactory career record, no hobbies, vacations in Tampa or Williamsburg, Virginia, a moderate drinker, no mistresses, and half a million dollars in unlisted bank accounts in the Cayman Islands.

Peterson and Roscoe and the others were easy to figure, had been easy to trace, too. They were careless and flashy, always showing up with a new car or Rolex watch, too eager to mention their vacations and new toys. They were the kind of cops who gave corruption a bad name. They annoyed him, but they would tumble soon enough. Their transgressions were routine and unimaginative—a little extortion and bribery. Roscoe was probably responsible for some of the cocaine that disappeared now and then from the evidence room, but Peterson wouldn't touch drugs.

Hollings and Wonton looked solid, and Barnes had never really been a suspect. Torrance remained the enigma.

The meeting ended. Wonton immediately plunged into a tale of their morning's adventure, liberally embellishing the facts so that by the time they got to the coffee machine, Wonton had actually jumped in the water and wrestled a great white with his bare hands to save three terrified *Sports Illustrated* swimsuit models.

"So—a little motion in the ocean this morning, huh?" Roscoe couldn't resist jibing as he passed Alex's office. "Tossed the old cookies, eh? Fed the fish?"

Alex forced his best good-natured smile. "Yeah, it was those eight-foot waves did me in. That and Wonton's old tugboat."

"Now, there's some truth—she's a fat old lady. Rolls like a son of a bitch."

"I hear you've got a sweet little number yourself."

"Sure do. Brand-new Donzi. Just picked it up last week. She'll do a hundred and ten with a tailwind."

"Maybe we can test out my stomach in a real boat."

"Damn right. But it's custom upholstery—you better know which way the wind's blowing."

Alex responded with the appropriate yuk-yuks and shut the door as Roscoe left. How could the guy be so brash about it? But it was a good invitation, a good in. He'd played the pal before, an easy role.

His coffee had gone cold and tasted bitter. He walked over to the window and poured the coffee on the rubber plant. This forlorn-looking plant had clung to its tenuous life through many years and a variety of caretakers. At times it had been loved and nurtured with regular doses of plant food, at other times it had been neglected to the point of collapse. Once it had been talked to. But nothing had ever made it healthy. This was a plant for a miser's grave.

Alex was not a plant person. The closest thing to a houseplant he had was growing in the back of the refrigerator in a long-forgotton bowl of leftover spaghetti. He didn't dislike foliage particularly, he just hadn't ever gotten used to the notion of domesticating it. But there it was when he arrived, with spotted leaves edged in brown and a minor plague of red bugs, so Alex had assumed its care by tossing it the dregs of his coffee every morning.

A hundred and ten MPH with a tailwind, he thought as he absently brushed a few of the bugs off one feeble leaf.

Chapter 3

Growing up around sailors on merchant ships had provided Chicago Nordejoong with a vivid lexicon of swear words. That evening as she sat below deck on the *Tassia Far,* the old wooden ketch she called home, she had already exhausted her regular vocabulary of oaths and was improvising new ones, aided by a bottle of bourbon. Her father's crews had come from around the world, and she could curse in dozens of languages. Right now she had run through Arabic, Greek, French, Norwegian, Spanish, and Korean.

As each new worry rose in her mind, she swore it down. It wasn't helping much. The loss of her skiff was the worst. That meant severe loss of income. Without the skiff, she couldn't collect fish or get to the other marinas where she often did repair work. Add to that the wound on her leg, which would keep her out of the water for a couple of weeks, just when she had a full scuba class ready to start their checkout dives. On top of that, the hospital bill would be expensive, and all in all, it didn't seem like that new mast would be a reality anytime soon.

She took another swallow from the bottle. She wasn't sure how dead-drunk was supposed to feel, but she didn't feel quite there yet and wasn't happy with it so far. The company of merchant seamen may have ruined her language, but it hadn't influenced her drinking. If anything, seeing the shore-night rum brawls and what staggering idiots the men could become had kept her away from liquor. But today had been so rotten it seemed like the thing to do.

She leaned back against the couch, nestling her body into its comforting bulk. It was a ridiculous thing to have on the boat, a huge antique with carved claw feet and horsehair stuffing. Her father had brought it from Brazil, the circumstances of possession never fully explained. Six men from the village were needed to carry it home from the dock. Her mother had just looked at it, shook her head, and sighed: "Dis monster going to break out de floor." They lived in Trinidad at the time, in a thatch house built on stilts. Her father dragged two trees in from the jungle and built supports under the floor where the couch would sit. The sofa was hoisted in with the aid of a block and tackle and a very confused burro.

Chicago sat up again, hissing the only oaths she knew in Polish, something about soot on your grandmother's stockings, as her injured leg slipped off the cushion. She pulled the chart closer, scrutinizing again the faint lines and markings that indicated Osprey Reef. The nautical markings and lines were getting blurry. Maybe she was a little drunk after all. But drunk or not, Chicago knew something was wrong out there.

Alex felt slightly out of place in the marina. When he first came to Miami he had sometimes visited the docks, but the world of pleasure boats was foreign to him. He liked the smell of varnish and salt, the sound of halyards clanking in the breeze. He was still attracted to the idea of sailing away someday. It seemed to him a perfect existence: calm, isolated, in tune with the world, and threatened only by nature and his own limits.

But now, as he walked along the wooden pier between moorings, he had a creepy feeling that all the vessels were alive and watching him, that they had heard about his ignoble defeat that morning and were snickering among themselves, somehow planning to kidnap him and take him out to the high seas, where they would toss him into an eternity of seasickness. He laughed as he remembered how rotten he had felt that morning. Yet he never got motion sickness from flying. Maybe he just needed more time on the water. Maybe it was just because he had been landlocked so long on the last assignment.

He found the *Tassia Far* in the end slip. It was an older boat, a wooden-hull ketch, forty-two feet long, a sleek design. It was a boat built to live on, but by someone who liked to move fast. The deck was immaculate and the waterline clean but there was no mast, and one sail, spread out on the aft deck, showed several patches.

Alex hesitated a moment, unsure of where to knock. Finally, he leaned over the stanchions, rapped on a hatch, and called toward the open companionway.

"Yeah—whaddaya want?" Chicago answered. She didn't sound particularly welcoming.

"Hello? It's, ah, Alex Sanders. We . . . met this morning," he responded somewhat awkwardly.

"Shit. Well, come on," he heard after a pause. Great, he thought, nice to be welcome. Alex climbed aboard and paused at the companionway entrance, looking down into the salon. He saw Chicago sitting on a huge overstuffed antique brocade couch, wearing a silk kimono, her bandaged leg elevated on a pile of cushions. Charts were spread on her lap and over a small table, which upon closer inspection proved to be the stuffed foot of an elephant.

"Come on," she repeated, but with a note of distrust and reluctance. Alex climbed down the teak ladder, ducking his head more than he had to, an instinct of the tall.

He glanced around and felt like he had stumbled somehow

into a weird movie set: *Tarzan Visits Lawrence of Arabia in a Junkyard on Jupiter.* There were woven tapestries and delicate watercolors hanging on the walls, as well as some vicious-looking jungle spears. There was a very authentic-looking shrunken head perched on the bleached pelvic bone of a large animal. A glass bowl full of fresh flowers rested on a hide-covered African drum.

Chicago looked smaller than he remembered. It must be the effect of the massive couch, he thought, and the frailty of bandages. She had to be five feet seven or eight. He hadn't seen her hair dry; it was straight and black and fell over her shoulders. On the table next to the charts was a nearly full can of condensed cream-of-mushroom soup with a spoon sticking out and a nearly empty bottle of Jack Daniels.

"I called the hospital. They gave me your address," he explained by way of openers. She didn't answer. "How's your leg?"

"Did you find out anything?" Chicago asked abruptly.

Alex was puzzled. "Find out what?"

"What! What do you mean what?" She sat up stiffly and swung her good leg to the floor. "What—what is going on at Osprey is what. Who the hell cut my anchor chain? What are you here for anyway?" She glared and then froze at the edge of the couch as if she would not move a muscle until he explained himself.

Alex, raised in the civility of the Midwest, thought that somehow she must be kidding, and of course she had had a stressful day. Perhaps this was her way of being friendly. He smiled.

"I thought I would just come see how you were doing. I couldn't stick around this morning."

"Oh well, I really missed you—damn near broke my heart. So did your buddy find out anything?"

"We didn't really know there was something to investigate. He filled out an incident report."

"Piss on your incidents! How can there be nothing to investigate? You're a cop. What the fuck did you do all day—write

jaywalking tickets on bluehairs?" Alex felt a ripple of apprehension, an automatic response that he quelled.

"How did you know I was a cop?"

"Umbi always knows that shit. He told me."

"That's your dive buddy, the one who disappeared?"

"So now you're asking questions? Bloody swell. We're attacked
by sharks and someone cuts my anchor line and escapes and
there's nothing to investigate?"

"Miss, uh, Nor-dejoung. [It was a definite handicap to have an
argument with someone whose name you couldn't even pro-
nounce.] The Dade County P.D. has no jurisdiction over rogue
marine life."

"You're funny as bait. So who cut my line? And where the hell
is my boat now?"

"I—ah don't know about the boat . . ."

"So what do you know?" she broke in angrily. "You know fish
piss in the ocean and it's hot in Miami! What is this, Donkey
Kong? You save the girl and end the game?" Chicago's hands
were clenched, and she pressed one against her stomach as if there
were a pain there. "What kind of crap do you investigate?" Her
eyes looked wild; her face, pinched and pale.

"Okay, wait a minute." The last vestiges of his grandmother's
hard-taught manners were about to snap. Alex didn't know what
to think, but he collected his own temper and bounded halfway
back up the ladder. "Let's try this again. Hi there, I'm friendly
Alex Sanders who pulled you out of the sea this morning, gal-
lantly saved your life, and graciously got you to the hospital. Just
came by to see how you were doing."

"You want a medal, buy Cracker Jacks. I didn't need no
shithead doctor sewing me up for eighteen dollars a stitch. You
think like an insurance company. Thanks for the rescue. I'll pay
the extra gas."

Alex was stunned. She didn't look like someone who was always so nasty, but it sure didn't seem they were going to hit it off and have a long and happy future together. He glanced at the bottle of bourbon. She didn't really sound drunk. He looked once again at the strange trappings in the cabin. Hell, maybe she was just a little nuts. At any rate, it had been a long day and he didn't need this shit. He turned to leave, then paused.

"Now, just for my own good—you know, like for the next time I might rescue someone from a feeding frenzy in the open sea—could you maybe tell me just what I did wrong? Just so I don't do it again, you understand."

"I didn't want to go to the hospital . . ."

"Then you should have said something before you fainted in the boat."

"I didn't faint," she snapped, but there was a childish defensiveness in the denial. "I—passed out."

"Fine, that's fainting."

"I was swimming for an hour! I was bleeding!"

Alex laughed. "So that's a good reason to faint, top-notch, I've done it myself."

"I didn't faint, and you can get the hell off my boat anyway, just go—go home and read your insurance policy or something. Get off my boat." Chicago was on the edge of the couch, and he had a vision of a leopard about to pounce. Her eyes were sparkling and she was shaking all over. He didn't know what he had done to engender such wrath, but he figured it was a good time to leave. He thought she might pull a blowgun out of the sleeve of her kimono and shoot him with poisoned darts.

"All right, okay." He backed off as if from a mad dog. "I'm going. I see why the shark only took one bite outta you!"

"I could've stitched it here! It's only skin. I have a kit for that, asshole! This is a boat! I know how to sew!" Alex wasn't quite making the connections in her reasoning but decided it was beyond him. "Why didn't you go after my boat! I . . ." As Alex reached the top of the ladder, he heard a soft thud. Chicago had fainted to the floor.

"She be drinking all the day."

Alex had lifted Chicago back onto the couch, determined she did indeed have blood in her veins and enough of a human heart to give it a pulse, and was trying to decide what to do when he heard the voice from the deck above. He turned at the sound of the voice and saw Umbi looking down through the companionway. He did not know how long he had been standing there, but from the amusement in his voice, Alex figured he had heard at least some of Chicago's tirade.

"She not much of a drinking lady, sir. But this not much of a good day, eh?" Umbi swung down into the salon with one graceful motion and held out his hand to Alex. "I thank you for taking us out that water—an' she too be grateful when she not so turned up inside." Umbi stepped over to the couch and touched the back of his hand to Chicago's face.

"She don't eat and she be havin' the coldness all day. That is from being close to killed. You know that feeling, sir?"

Alex nodded. "Is she always this mean?"

"Oh, no." Umbi seemed eager to defend his friend. "It's only when she . . . repress her anxiety so." Alex must have looked puzzled. "Oprah Winfrey talk about dat," Umbi added, as if that explained everything.

"Right." Alex nodded. "So how are you doing?" Umbi had disappeared that morning as soon as Wonton got them to shore.

"Oh, I be feelin' that anxiety." He did look a little strung out, Alex thought. "I tell you that. But I don't have no bite out of me."

"You're okay then?"

Umbi shrugged and smiled. "I think I like to stay on top of the water for a while."

Alex smiled his agreement. Umbi seemed a little uneasy. Of course, Alex thought—I'm a cop, he's probably an illegal alien and a minor. Alex stepped away, slumped his shoulders a little, sank into a chair, and made himself smaller to put the boy at ease. He glanced at Chicago. She looked so gentle now, her face tranquil, her black hair spread across the bright pillow. A little color had come back into her face.

"I thought shark attacks were really pretty rare."

"Ain't rare enough," Umbi said quietly, and a shudder darted through his thin body.

"Chicago thinks someone cut your anchor line." Alex changed the subject, sensing Umbi's discomfort.

"Yeah, I think it's true. It don't break itself and it don't pull out. We check it first thing down."

"Who would cut it?"

"We hear a boat at one time and try to look for it, but dat's when all the shit go on the fan."

"Is Chicago her real name?"

"I don't know no other."

"What do you know?" Alex persisted. Humberto gazed at him suspiciously.

"She good friend for me. She find me work and give me books to read. She good at fixing tings. She want to fix this boat up and sail away."

"Where is she from?"

"Her father a ship captain an' he build this boat. I think he's from Norway or Sweden, up there. Her mother from Trinidad, but she dead." He gestured to the tapestries on the wall and the woven pillows scattered around the salon. "Chicago make these cloths. She have this"—Umbi stalled on the word, made the motions of a loom—"cloth weaver back there." He gestured toward the aft cabin. "She terrible cook. She don't care she eat like this all the time!" He waved a scornful hand at the can of cold soup.

Umbi shrugged. "I don't know what to tell you, mon, she my friend."

Chicago stirred restlessly, her breathing quickened, and they heard soft cries. Umbi went to the couch and pulled a blanket over her, pressing it down around her. "See now, you ain't in the water no more. See now, you back home," he comforted.

Chapter 4

Alex brushed at a bee that was hovering persistently over his bouquet of carnations. "Shoo, ya little fucker!" he hissed at the blooms, then smoothing his smile back on like honey on a biscuit, he turned toward a matronly trio walking down the sidewalk.

"Sanctified church of the eternal golden way . . ." The ladies arched away and quickened their pace, clutching their pocketbooks and casting frowns of disapproval.

". . . his glorious incarnated Swami Raja Daja Do Dah bestows his seven levels of blessing upon you anyway," he called after the escaping figures. "And have a NICE day!"

Alex glanced down the alley behind him. Still no activity. It was almost three o'clock. These sandals were hard to stand around in, and his nose was feeling sunburned. Good thing I decided not to join the Moonies after all, he thought. A banker type in a gray suit approached, briefcase in hand, carefully avoiding eye contact.

"Please, sir, spread the message of joy . . ." Alex held out a carnation to the man and was stunned when, without missing a step or even glancing at him, the banker slipped a dollar bill into his hand before he even got to the Swami Raja Daja part. Alex stared at the bill in disbelief.

"Thank you! Oh thank you, sir!" he called hastily after the

man. "Oh, your flower, hey! You're supposed to get a flower!" Oh well. He shrugged and turned the bill over a few times, like a kid who had just sold his first lemonade. What to do with it? What department regulation covered this sort of thing? He slipped the bill into the baggy trousers and turned back to his proselytizing with renewed zeal.

At ten minutes to four, the truck pulled up to the back door of the fish market. It was a small refrigerated truck with REDONDO CO-OP and a friendly smiling lobster painted on the side. Alex lay his bouquet down on top of the *Miami Herald* vending machine and knelt down to buckle his sandal. By the time he recovered the bouquet, Wonton and Detective Melissa Barnes were already on their way across the street.

Wonton wore plaid Bermuda shorts and a checkered sport shirt, and Melissa's hair was sprayed into something vaguely resembling a baked ham. Barnes was a compact woman of forty-six with assisted but not glaring auburn hair. She was trim but on the stocky side. She had been in vice for eight years and was a good investigator, a detail person valuable and creative in planning undercover operations. She didn't participate often—her five-feet-two physique made her too memorable—but this fish market stakeout seemed a sure, if minor, event.

At four o'clock Wonton and Barnes entered Reggi's Fish Market and began to argue over the price of pompano. A few minutes later a charcoal-gray 1988 Camaro pulled up in front of the fish market and Alex watched as Caron Morales and an unknown man got out.

Morales was a slender man of average height who carried himself with regal gracefulness. He dressed well and his grooming was impeccable, but he was homely. His face was round and pouchy in the cheeks. His nose was long, his lips thin, his chin missing. He had small, feminine hands.

But none of this seemed to bother him. Anyway, he was rich enough to buy affection. His partner of the moment was much younger, Caucasian, with light brown hair, perhaps twenty-five. He looked a little nervous. Seeing them together out to lunch, one might have thought them mentor and junior executive.

In the world of legitimate business, Morales would be considered mid-level management. In the world of cocaine distribution and in Alex Sanders's esteem, he was considered mid-level scum. Morales was a judicious dealer of modest life-style. He had not succumbed to the flashy cars, extravagant trappings, and lust for power that had toppled other dealers. He had invested his profits in real estate, bonds, office buildings, and a retirement community in West Palm Beach.

He controlled enough territory to command the respect of his local street dealers but was small enough not to be a threat to the kingpins. He was elusive and clever. He knew, and the cops knew, that prosecuting him would be a long and difficult affair, with shaky evidence, numerous appeals, and a minimal sentence —a lot of police work for a relatively minor fish.

Alex despised drug dealers and he despised mediocrity, so he doubly despised Morales. Whenever he thought of Morales, he longed for the Middle Ages. As soon as the two men entered the store, Alex untied the purple scarf from around his neck and stuffed it into the woven bag he carried over one shoulder. At that signal, two unmarked police cars shifted into position at either end of the street.

"Larry, two pounds is enough. This ain't the only time in her life your cousin Mavis is gonna eat shrimp. We don't have to roll out the red carpet all the way down the street!" Detective Barnes whined and glanced up as Morales entered the shop. "I gotta eat hamburger," she continued without missing a beat. "Me and the kids eat hamburger and you gotta be the big shot for Mavis so her husband will get you a good deal on a Toyota."

"He sells more than just Toyotas," Wonton woofed a reply. "Why don't you just shut up and let's get this done. We gotta buy cheese and crackers and stuff."

"I don't like cheese. You don't like cheese. What're we gonna do, sit around and pretend like we like cheese for Mavis?"

"I like cheese." Wonton winked at Reggi, the fish market owner. Reggi tapped his fingers impatiently on the counter.

"You like Velveeta," Melissa snipped. "He likes Velveeta," she repeated to the two men as she turned away from her "husband" in a huff and opened her purse. She rummaged around, slipped the safety off her gun, and held the purse with the clasp undone. Morales and his partner ignored them, gazing impassively at the display cases.

"What are these ones here again?" Wonton pointed to one lane of shrimp resting on ice.

Reggi sighed. "Those are twenty-to-thirty-twos. Four ninety-five a pound."

"And that's what? I mean, you say it's the size, but it's what, length? Is that inches or centimeters or what? I don't get it."

"Larry, this fish stuff is too much trouble." Melissa pushed her glasses up in a gesture of puzzlement. Why couldn't Morales and his buddy just make their purchase and let themselves get caught?

"Pounds," Reggi snapped. "It's, ah, how many in a pound. These are twenty to thirty-two in a pound, those are sixteen to twenty."

"Larry, I know how many ounces are in a pound and it don't change like that." Reggi glanced at the two new customers. "I'll be right with you." They smiled and nodded.

"Dummy, you're thick! You're so thick." He gave Reggi one of his best exasperated man-to-man looks. "How much are those, the sixteen-to-twenties?"

"Six seventy-five." Reggi wasn't pushing for a sale.

"Oh well, Larry, that doesn't seem right. You get more with those ones. These cost more and they give you less. I told you we should have gone to Variety . . ."

"Stupid, those are bigger, you get more shrimp, they ain't cheating you."

Wonton was loving it. Always knew he was sit-com material.

Barnes was making notes to herself for the next squad meeting: Why did the wife always have to be the dumb one?

They continued bickering, hoping to force Morales to make his buy, but the two men just leaned against the wall and quietly observed a row of flounder. Finally, it was Reggi who forced their hand.

"Look, I tell you what I'm gonna do. You got the pompano, right, here's the pompano!" He grabbed the fish by the tails and slapped them on the scale. "You say Variety has 'em for five twenty-five. Fine. I sell them for five twenty-five. You want Mavis to have a nice time? Look, here's the shrimp—sixteen-to-twenties for the price of the little guys." He scooped a load of the shrimp into the paper without even weighing them. "See—it's all done. Go buy your cheese. You want a new Toyota—take mine. Here's the keys!" Reggi slammed his keys down on the counter. "Just get the hell out of my store!"

Wonton paid for the fish and took the bag. He considered stalling over cash or charge, but it seemed all the stalling in the world wasn't going to force the buy.

As Wonton and Barnes started for the door, a relieved Reggi turned to his new customers. "Yes, sir, what can I do for you!"

"Would you have any sushi-grade tuna?" they heard as the door closed behind them. "Yellowfin, preferably. And I'll need a lot. I'm throwing a rather large party . . ."

Wonton glanced toward Alex and shook his head slightly, then he and Barnes slipped up against the next building, just out of view of the plate-glass window in Reggi's fish shop.

In less than two minutes, Morales and his partner swung open the door, each with two large packages wrapped in white leak-proof paper. It was good quality, too, the heavy stuff, not that flimsy second-rate butcher paper they used at Variety. Barnes broke off three of her press-on nails tearing open the generous bag of sixteen-to-twenty-size shrimp they had purchased. Just as Morales left the shop, Wonton and Barnes stepped in their path. They collided in an explosion of shrimp, spilling a slippery carpet of crustaceans all over the sidewalk.

Wonton had his gun out. "Freeze, police!" he boomed. His favorite line, delivered like Othello, Alex thought as he dove down into the baggy pants to retrieve his own gun from its leg holster. The younger man slipped and fell to the sidewalk in a splatter of shrimp, staring unbelievingly into the barrel of Barnes's little .38 Smith & Wesson.

Morales tried to run and stepped square on a fat shrimp. (Must have been one of them number sixteens, Wonton later decided.) He slipped, he staggered, his arms flapped, then he crashed through the plate-glass window and landed face first in an artistic display of fresh raw octopus, sending up a little fountain of crushed ice.

Alex took off down the alley after Reggi, who had escaped out the back door, and grabbed him before he cleared the second Dumpster. "Hey, buddy," Alex said as he slammed him up against the green metal with a satisfying thud. "Let me tell you about the sanctified truth of the eternal golden way. You have the right to remain silent . . ."

It was a triumphant, if fishy, trio that trooped into the station after depositing Morales, Reggi, and Hugo Sims, the young accomplice, in the tank.

"So when's the fish fry?" Wonton asked as he plopped down in a swivel chair by Alex's desk. "We still got the pompano and half the shrimp."

"What did you do, pick it up off the sidewalk?" Barnes asked.

"Only the ones that hadn't been stepped on," Wonton explained. "C'mon, they've got shells! I'll rinse 'em off. A little garlic, white wine . . ."

"Isn't that, perhaps, evidence?" she pointed out as she kicked her cheap, chunky shoes off.

"No, the tuna's evidence. That is definitely evidence," Wonton admitted, patting the thick package. The cocaine Morales had come to buy had been stuffed inside the tuna's gutted belly. "And who needs tuna anyway? That sushi crap is for liberals. But the rest isn't evidence, it's . . . props—yeah, that's it—props. Just like those shoes and Alex's little hippie pants."

"Speaking of which, who does wardrobe around here these days?" Barnes complained. "I can't be wearing stuff like this. My feet have been around too long. And this polyester makes my skin crawl."

"Hey, I may dress like this from now on." Alex held out the baggy pants and flapped the sides like a skirt. There was a jingling in his pocket. "Oh yeah, I almost forgot!"

Wonton and Barnes looked on open-mouthed as Alex emptied the contents of the capacious pockets and the woven bag out onto the table and began to count the surprise booty of his undercover afternoon.

"Thirteen dollars and twenty-one cents. I might just quit the force and get religion," Wonton marveled, running his fingers over the pile of change and occasional crumpled dollar bill.

"That goes on report," Captain Torrance's voice broke into their gaity. "Under incidental procurements."

"Captain, you're kidding. You're kidding, right?" Wonton leapt out of the chair and lay his arm like a fallen log across the captain's shoulders. "We're risking life and limb, exposing our- selves to constant peril, and some kind citizens find it in their hearts to contribute a few pennies to a noble cause!"

"On the report."

"Captain, it was a clean bust! We've got Morales and who knows what other new leads. This is hardly enough for a round of cheap beer, and you know Alex don't even drink that stuff. He likes those fancy kinds with little scribbles and seals all over the labels. Why, Captain, this won't even pay for the soap to wash the fish stink off our hands," Wonton protested.

"Try lemon juice," the captain offered. "But the pompano are yours. My wife has a great recipe. If you like, I could call her and get it for you."

"Gee thanks, Captain."

"Anything for my team." Torrance smiled, trying a little too hard to participate in the levity. Humor didn't really become him. While the captain was generally liked, he was not, as Willy Loman had also failed to be, *well* liked. He had that slightly pathetic social awkwardness that made people a little uncomfort- able. People couldn't name anything about him they didn't like; it was just, well, he was on the dull side. He was no one you would necessarily pick to go out for a beer with; and probably never had been. Meeting him at a party you wouldn't try to avoid him, but after exchanging greetings and talking about golf or business for a few minutes, you would be at a loss for what to say next.

Torrance was a little over six feet tall but seemed smaller. He was built of squares and planes. His shoulders were square to his hips, his face was square, framed by a square gray hairline. Even the bald spot on the back of his head was shaped like a cocktail napkin. He was fit for a man in his fifties, with a flabless boxy torso. His hands were large, the palms like snow shovels. They seemed to pull on his arms, causing his shoulders to slump.

Captain Alton Torrance left them with his congratulations and a pile of paperwork. The levity was soon subdued under the pile of arrest forms and reports. Alex was halfway through trying to estimate the number of shrimp on the sidewalk at the time of arrest when Mrs. James Beaufort popped her head into his office.

Mrs. James Beaufort had worked as a secretary with the Dade County police force for forty-two years and had never been called anything but Mrs. James Beaufort. They had held a betting pool once to guess her first name, but that was before Alex had come and he had never thought to inquire. Nothing else could fit her anyway.

"Detective Sanders sir, a woman came to see you at four-oh-five this afternoon, while you were still participating in your undercover assignment," Mrs. James Beaufort announced in a soft, old-family Southern accent. Her face was bright, her smile open and benign, like Andy Griffith's. "She regretted she could not wait for you to return, but she did leave a brief letter. I just wanted to make sure you found it."

Alex scanned the desk and lifted stacks of paper. He hadn't seen any letter. "I didn't notice anything when we came in. What did she look like, ma'am?" Alex asked absently as he reviewed their triumphant entrance. He recalled that Wonton had dropped the wet bag of fish carelessly on the edge of his blotter. Now, he flipped through the trash and saw, stuck to the soggy paper, an equally soggy paper.

"Oh well, she was taller than me . . . [which was above five feet four] and she was pretty, but in a—a rugged [this word tumbled out with a note of relief, as if Mrs. James Beaufort had searched desperately for some polite phrasing] sort of way. You know, pretty like those women in the *National Geographic* who study chimpanzees and dig up skeletons. Pretty, but in need of some lotions." She paused for a moment, not in thought—for Mrs. James Beaufort had meticulous recall—but for the most generous phrasing. "She had straight hair—that was the most striking thing. It was black and long like those ladies' in those tropical paintings, the ones from the island where that painter who died of leprosy lived."

Alex barely supressed a laugh.

"Oh, and she walked with a cane, but I don't think she always does. She didn't look like one who habitually requires assistance."

"Mrs. James Beaufort, you are remarkably astute." Alex rose as the elderly lady smiled and waved a gloved goodbye. He unfolded the soggy note. The ink was blurred but readable.

"I came over to apologize. I am very sorry for my rudeness last week. If you ever need something fixed on your boat, please come see me. Chicago."

For someone with so much to say in person she's unusually abrupt on paper, Alex thought as he spread the page out to dry in a drawer.

Chapter 5

Alex was not one to fuss over clothing. He had a natural easiness of posture that made anything he wore seem right, a good sense of color, and four sisters with good taste in presents.

Yet as he showered he was wondering what he should wear for his second visit, or attempted visit, to the *Tassia Far*. Camouflage and pith helmet? Mandarin wizard's robe? Maybe something in goatskin. He spied a pair of khaki pants draped across a chair and went for their worn-in comfort, even at the risk of looking like a casual young lawyer.

The shirt was a little trickier. Alex had a personal boycott against polo shirts, with their snobby little collars and logos, and most of his T-shirts declared something. Although they were mostly inoffensive declarations, mentioning some bicycle race or other, there was no way to tell what might offend Chicago Nordejoong. Maybe a bicycle once crushed her pet spider, he thought as he flipped through the hangers.

Ah, perfect—a dark blue cotton shirt, handwoven in Guatemala. He liked the shirt but didn't wear it too often. Alex was six feet tall (exactly, and never stretched it to six-one) and muscular. The Guatemalans were small people, and even though he had had the shirt custom made in the fairly touristed town of Chichicastenango, the tailor didn't seem to be able to think in broad enough terms. The shirt was just a little too snug for police work and a little to nice for knocking around in.

If she doesn't judo me to the floor, it'll be just fine, he thought as he tucked it in.

Chicago was sitting on deck when Alex arrived. He stopped a few boats away and watched her. It was dusk, the soft purplish dusk that seems to wash up from the bottom of the sea. She sat with her back to him, looking out over the bay. A piece of cloth that she had been embroidering now lay idle in her lap. This small neglected piece of needlework made the scene tranquil. She wore a faded blouse and a bright sarong for a skirt. She looked lost in the ease of twilight—suspended and thoughtful. Alex felt almost intrusive

Making his footsteps heard so as not to startle her, Alex walked just past the *Tassia Far* to the edge of the dock and paused there before turning around to face her.

"Hello again."

"Hello."

He couldn't see her face well, but her voice sounded a little startled.

"I, uh, I don't have much of a pretext here," Alex explained with his usual easy candor. "I just thought I'd come see you. I got your note."

"I should have come over sooner," Chicago broke in. "I really am sorry."

"No, that's okay. It was . . . ah, interesting to meet you."

She laughed. "Umbi said I was horrible."

"No—well, actually yes."

Chicago stood up in the cockpit as if centering herself in her world, one hand on the helm. Alex stood on the dock, looking down the row of masts like a forest of straight trees framed against the Miami skyline.

"How is your leg?"

"It's fine. Thank you."

"Good, that's good."

Finally, with a shyness he would never have expected, Chicago invited him aboard. They sat in the cockpit, on opposite sides, buffered by the darkness.

"I meant it about your boat. I can tune it up or something," Chicago offered.

"Oh, it's not my boat. It belongs to my partner. I was just along for the experience."

"You're not from Miami, are you?"

Alex laughed. "North Dakota. About as far from any ocean as you can get."

"That's the Midwest?" Alex wondered for a second if she was joking, then remembered what Umbi had told him of her history.

"The exact geographical center of North America."

"Did you live on a farm? With animals and stuff? Like cows?" Chicago asked.

"Oh yeah. Lots of cows."

"I've always thought them so bizarre. The most absurd creatures, in a glorious sort of way. So slow and square. And then you milk them." Pause. A fish jumped nearby; an elderly man puttered by in a dinghy. Alex tried to sort out the cows but gave up. She had no specific accent, but there was a different kind of cadence to her speech. It was as if she left sentences with the edges slightly bent.

"Umbi said you've lived on boats most of your life."

"Dad was a merchant captain. He's Norwegian. My mother was from Trinidad. We lived there until I was around five. He would sail around for a few months, then stay with us a few months. When she died, I went to sea with him. I'm afraid it ruined my language," she added with chagrin.

"You must have seen a lot of the world."

"Yeah." She pulled at a thread in her hem.

"Did you like it?"

"The world?"

Alex laughed. "Yeah."

Chicago smiled and looked at him. She couldn't see his face well—he was silhouetted by the lamp on the end of the pier—but she liked the shape of him, the way he sort of sprawled his arms across the cushion back. She liked the way he took up space without squashing it.

"Yeah—it's a pretty good world. Have you traveled much?"

"A little." Alex brushed the question aside. "I guess you get asked this a lot . . ."

"My name?" Chicago laughed. Alex felt relieved at the lightness of the sound. "Mom had never been off the island. Somewhere she had heard about Chicago, had a picture of it from a magazine or something, and thought it was this great romantic American kingdom."

"You're lucky she didn't read about Wichita Falls or Buffalo."

Chicago laughed, then a shadow of something caught the laugh and it closed.

"So, do you still have family back there?" she asked.

"Oh yeah, my parents, grandmother, two of my sisters and their families, a few dozen assorted cousins. It was a large family. There were my four sisters and me in one house, then my aunt next door, with eight boys and one girl. The parents eventually gave up trying to sort out who belonged where and settled for a nightly head count." He felt the usual twinge of pain to think of his family. He hadn't been home for almost four years now. Too risky. At least now they knew he was alive.

"Sounds like that Norman Rockwell sort of thing."

"Oh, no." Alex laughed. "Dali, maybe. Old Norman would have run in horror. My mother raised bugs, my grandmother was an anarchist, and my oldest sister raced motorcycles. When Dad wasn't farming, he was an inventor, specializing in explosions, and half my uncles were in a flying circus . . ."

"True?"

Alex nodded, a little surprised to find himself running on like that. The night grew cool. They began to talk easily. Perhaps it's a good idea to have a knock-down drag-out fight upon first meeting, just to get it out of the way.

Chicago invited him below. The cabin looked friendlier this time. The disarray was gone, the lights were soft. In the light, Chicago noticed his shirt and reached instinctively to touch the fabric. Alex was surprised. (Damn, it's a hackneyed line, but there was a thrill at her touch, he admitted to himself later.)

"It's lovely!" she exclaimed, then drew her hand back as if she had committed a trespass.

"Yeah, well, my loincloth is at the cleaner's."

Chicago laughed and glanced around the cabin. She so rarely had new visitors that she forgot how it must look to a stranger.

"It's from Guatemala? Have you been there?"

"Uh, a friend brought it back." She looked at him, caught his hesitation, but let it pass.

Another pause. "So who's your decorator?" Alex said.

"It's just stuff from along the way. Dad liked to get off the ship and hang out with the natives. He would play cards or dominoes and win this stuff."

"Is this him?" Alex picked up a photograph. "And you?" A tall man with thick reddish-blond hair and beard was sitting in the wooden skeleton of a hull with a hammer in his hand and a disassembled something spread around him while a child sat nearby chewing on a ratchet wrench. Now he understood her unusual combination of features. Her eyes, a light color between blue and gray, were from the Norwegian side, her hair from the islands. She had inherited some of her father's height and boniness, but in Chicago this was smoothed over with the hint of voluptuousness that he associated with Caribbean women.

"Yeah, that was taken in Trinidad. He was just building the *Tassia Far.*"

"What does the name mean?" Alex asked. Chicago took the picture from him and brushed a smudge from the frame.

"It was supposed to be the *Tassia Fair,* after my mother. He had *Tassia F* already painted when she died."

"Where is he now?" Alex asked.

"Easter Island, I think. South Pacific, anyway. Captaining one of these new exploration cruise ship deals." There was another pause, but even the pauses were getting more comfortable.

"Well, sit down anyway," Chicago offered. "Do you want some tea?"

"Sure, yes," Alex accepted, then immediately had a queasy regret, suspicious about the possible herbs and barks she might brew. He sat on the sofa and glanced over the row of books tucked neatly into a niche. He pulled out a volume on celestial navigation and flipped through it. Chicago filled the kettle and lit the propane burner, then glanced up.

"Um, Alex, do you like snakes?"

"Excuse me?" Alex wasn't sure he had heard her correctly.

"I just didn't want you to be startled," Chicago explained as she knelt on the sofa next to him. She smelled of cloves and a touch of WD40. "She's perfectly harmless," she continued as she reached over him and pulled out a couple more volumes. A fist-size clearly reptilian head poked slowly out from behind the books, flicking its forked tongue in the air.

"Oh sure, yeah, actually how stupid of me not to expect a couple." Snakes did not bother Alex, and this one was quite beautiful; still, it was not what he had been expecting to find on her bookshelf.

"We got set up to smuggle exotic birds and reptiles once, years and years ago. They were packed inside crates of ceramics from Venezuela. Some of the birds died and started to stink, so we found it out. We let them all go when we got to Panama. You should have seen that! Fifty-some parrots flying off at once. We let the snakes go at night. But this one was banged up." Chicago lifted the snake from its hiding place. It was an eight-foot-long red-tailed boa constrictor. "She was blind and sort of kinked in two places, here and here. So we kept her."

"Nice." Alex admired the snake, casually scratching the top of its head. "What's her name?"

"Actually, I don't know if it's a him or a her, but the name is Lassie. I really wanted a dog at the time. But I love you, dearie." She spoke to the huge reptile with all the affection of the silliest cat owner. Chicago made the tea and brought a mug to Alex. It smelled normal. She moved down to the other end of the couch, absently pulling her legs up. Alex saw the scar, still red and raw-looking, crescent-shaped. She noticed this and pulled the hem of her sarong over it.

"I took the stitches out this morning." She shrugged.

"Nice scar. Kind of dramatic."

"Now, let's talk about this shark business," Chicago seized the opening. "There really is something strange going on out there. First of all, sharks don't just attack like that . . ."

Alex groaned to himself. He was finding the sofa really comfortable and had just noticed that when she moved, her sarong tended to slip up a little on the silky brocade. Alex's mind was not on the strange occurrences at Osprey Reef.

Chapter 6

"They bounced Morales." Wonton strode into Alex's office with no overture, slamming the door behind him.

"No chance. How could they, anyway?"

"He didn't even spend the weekend in jail. Judge Selby got called away from the Saturday morning breakfast special at Denny's to sign the release."

"What's the deal?"

"Don't know. I'm on my way to see the captain now. Thought you and the ASPCA might like to come along."

"Let's go," Alex said bitterly as he got up.

Torrance was expecting them. Wonton entered with his usual bluster, swinging a truncheon of verbal abuse. Alex was more restrained. He simply stood by the doorway, a disquieting silent presence, his body seemingly at ease but with the coiled ease of a gunfighter. Torrance glanced at him and felt a flicker of something, an uneasy recognition, a suggestion for the first time that this mild-tempered farm-boy cop had more in his past than playing tuba in the high school marching band.

"I was expecting you," Torrance said simply.

"Invitation must've got lost in the mail," Wonton snapped. On the force twenty years, Wonton was more familiar with Torrance.

He dragged a chair close to his desk, straddled it, picked a pen out of a holder, and began to doodle on his blotter.

"We traded up." The captain got right to the point. "Morales has lines on all the big boys. I don't like it any more than you do, but I'd rather see Garcia or Kalispel fall."

"Why so fast? *How* so fast?" Wonton interrupted. "He wasn't in the can long enough to piss there!"

"Morales has connections, you know that," the captain replied irritably. "He owns more lawyers than BMW. He has too many legitimate connections and business concerns."

Like the $11 million South Beach Plaza development in which Judge Selby holds a large stock percentage, Alex thought to himself.

"So what's the deal?" Wonton persisted. "If he's got all those hotshot lawyers, why would he squeal over something like this? Face it, chief, it was a nice bust, but it ain't that big. They could have him out in a couple days anyway."

"One of the ways Morales has been able to flourish as a small fish in a big pond is by keeping careful track of his competition. He's got dirt on everyone. Provable dirt. We made a deal. Morales turns over his files and testifies; he walks and we've got the Garcia brothers and possibly even Dominic Kalispel."

Wonton dropped the pen onto the desk and got up. He walked over to the window shaking his head. "I don't like it. The guy is slimy. And what can he have on Kalispel? He's like a fly in Kalispel's pigpen."

"We had two years of undercover work and God knows how many backstage hours into our last attempt on Kalispel"—there was a twinge of irritation in Torrance's voice—"and you know what happened."

"Yeah." Wonton grunted.

Alex said nothing. He knew what had happened to foul the

Kalispel investigation. He knew what had appeared to happen, and he was pretty sure he knew what had really happened.

"I guess you're right," Wonton offered reluctantly. "And even if you're not, it looks like there isn't a fucking thing we can do about it now anyway."

Alex's face didn't change expression, but he felt a cold thud in his stomach. Wonton was giving in too easily.

"But how can we trust Morales to come through?" Wonton asked.

"We have to trust him."

"No we don't." Alex finally spoke up. "He's dead by now or out of the country. But probably dead."

"We have him under police protection."

"You think that means anything?" Alex felt his temper rising and his voice coming out rough. He felt a pounding in his ears and wanted to smash Torrance against the wall. He controlled himself, pulled his voice back to casual.

"Word gets out that Morales is busted, then the next day he shows up for bagels at Wolfies. It wouldn't take a genius to figure out he made a deal." Alex shrugged.

"Detective Sanders." Torrance was trying for the slightly paternal yet kind tone, but he just sounded annoyed. "You are new to Miami. You have a reputation as a good cop, but there are realities about this business that continue to escape you. I could arrest a dozen petty dealers every day, line them up, and shoot them, and it wouldn't make a difference. We need to get the kingpins. Dominic Kalispel runs one of the most productive drug-shipping organizations on the East Coast. If trading in one petty middleman for a chance at Kalispel has a chance, I'm willing to take it. Besides" —his voice took on a steely edge—"Morales will get his sooner or later." There was a thick silence in the office.

"What about Morales's young partner, Sims? And the fish market guy?" Wonton broke in.

"Sims is just one of Morales's hired hands—new to the game, hasn't got much of a record. He's nothing. We'll keep him. Sam Reggiano, the fish market owner, has no record, claims he never knew what was in the fish. Claims Morales came in a few months ago, told him he was a restaurant owner, and needed a good source for sushi-grade tuna. Surprise: A few days later someone from the Redondo Co-op shows up and offers to supply him regularly. Reggi is a smart businessman. He's got Morales's card; he arranges to have twenty pounds available every Friday. Claims he never unwrapped the fish, claims the five-hundred-a-week fee is a 'retainer' to ensure that the fish are always the best and never sold to the competition. Totally innocent."

"Saint Peter ain't that innocent," Wonton interjected scornfully.

"Saint Peter isn't that smart, either, or he wouldn't still be vice-god," Alex pointed out.

"I'm sorry," Torrance continued, "but with no record, a good lawyer, and a clean suit, he'll be back overpricing pompano in a few days."

Wonton shrugged and started for the door. "Case closed, then. What say we go chase pickup trucks with missing mudflaps—hey!" he suggested sarcastically to Alex.

"I'd like the rest of the day off, captain, if I could."

Torrance stared at him for a moment. "We don't need any hotshot bullshitting . . ."

"No, sir. It's just . . . I need a ride, personal leave."

Chapter 7

Alex slammed the Morales files into his desk, locked the drawers, and poured the cold dregs of his morning coffee into the rubber plant. It was looking healthy lately. Maybe coffee was what it had needed all along. Five minutes later he had changed into bicycle shorts and T-shirt, laced up his cycling shoes, and slung his racing helmet over one arm. He strode down the hall wishing for something to knock over. He retrieved his bicycle from the basement and sprinted up the steps with it, so angry he almost crashed into Mrs. James Beaufort, who was just returning from lunch. She stopped and stared at him, a wrinkle in her usual propriety, one gloved hand resting on the stair rail, the other pressed to her bosom.

Alex nodded and apologized, still distracted and too tense to notice her surprise.

"Why, Detective Sanders," she blurted, her attention drawn to his black lycra cycling attire. "I've never seen you wearing such nice muscles—oh, ah, shorts." She blushed at her slip, and one gloved hand flew to her mouth as she hurried up the stairs. Alex laughed; some threads of anger slipped. He swung onto the bicycle and slipped into the toe clips.

He rode impatiently through the city, squeezing through red lights and weaving between cars in a manner that he would usually stop younger riders for and deliver a stern lecture against. He was mad. It just didn't fit. There was something going on and he couldn't figure it. Torrance was up to something; now he was beginning to doubt Wonton as well.

He turned on to Route 1, where the straight, flat highway rolled south to the edge of the continent, luring him to escape. The city yielded slowly, panning out in a series of Burger Kings, Wendy's, and the other burger places; low, flat shopping malls with one or another discount warehouse; used-car lots with no deals. There was something innately tiring about the stretch, as if everything had grown old and thin and had just laid down. Alex rode hard, crouched over the handlebars, bent in concentration.

Ten miles outside Miami, he clicked into the pace. Pedaling became a rhythm, a mantra, and all that existed were man and machine, muscles and wheels: no obstacles. The sensation was intoxicating, overpowering. Riding like this gave Alex the feeling that nothing was out of reach, that all he had to do was keep the concentration and power going and he would reach the edge and sail off.

He trained now. He knew about pacing and physiology and electrolyte imbalances, but as a boy he used to ride until he quite literally sailed off the edge. His first ten-speed came to him through a catalog, hard earned from haying. While his friends were thrashing out the vicissitudes of adolescence in the time-ordained rituals of the late sixties—driving fast, drinking hard, and trying whatever drugs managed to make their way to their rural corner of the world—Alex got addicted to riding. North Dakota was a vast flat world with endless horizons to a boy of fourteen, and he became obsessed with moving across them.

He began to take long rides without stopping, seeing how much farther he could go each time. The roads there were uninterrupted, straight, and flat; he could go forever. It was his first taste of pure motion, speed, and self-powered freedom. One day he rode for his usual twenty or so miles, then he didn't turn around, didn't let up even when his body began to ache and his chest was pounding. It was late summer and the sky was dry and distant.

He began to feel a strange sensation, an exhilaration, a displacement, a drunkenness that surpassed by far his feeble experiments with beer and pot. The road hummed and his mind hummed and he couldn't stop. He rode as hard as he could for as long as he could and even then he didn't stop until he passed out.

Alex woke up in a field of wheat; he had rolled down an embankment. The furrow cradled his body and the sun beat down on his face and he could hear the wheat rustling in the wind. Everything shimmered and his senses seemed turned up and on fire. When, a few years later, he tried a hit of acid with his cousin, he recognized the feeling. A farmer saw his bike on the roadway and stopped; drove Alex forty miles back to Brownsville, then called his father to pick him up and take him the rest of the way, another thirty miles.

It began to be a regular occurrence—farmers, truckers, state police, once a Greyhound bus, bringing the boy home, weak and shaky, half tranced. It worried his mother; the relatives conferred. She locked up the bicycle, made him see the doctor, talked to the minister. Alex couldn't explain, couldn't stop. Lottie, his favorite older sister, would find him gone, escaped somehow, despite the family's best efforts, and drive off to find him.

"Alex, couldn't you at least turn around at fifty miles or so, so you wind up near the farm at the end?" she suggested. But he couldn't explain. It was the endlessness he craved. Lottie dated a highway patrolman for a while and for a while did manage to get Alex stopped and turned around so he would collapse at least within a twenty-mile radius of the farm; but when the couple broke up, it was straight lines again.

He rode to Montana. He rode to Minnesota and South Dakota.

He rode to Canada, oblivious to the border crossing, and the guards chased him down and held him overnight in jail.

Finally, Grandma came to his rescue. Told Uncle Jerry, a crop duster and flying-circus pilot, to teach the boy to fly.

Today he rode to Key Largo. He stopped at a little store, re-filled his water bottle, and drank from it slowly as he paced around in the shade stretching his muscles. Then Alex went to the pay phone on the porch outside, dialed the long-distance operator, and waited for his connection.

"Lieutenant Braddock's office."

"Sanders here."

"One moment, sir." Alex listened as the call was transferred to Braddock's special line.

"Alex! How's the tropics?"

"Hot."

"And the project?"

"Just warming up. All our starting players are definitely in the game. I need rundowns on some new ones." Alex gave him the names; hesitated.

"That all?"

"No, uh, one more—Detective Frank Baxter. Alias Wonton."

"Are you into anything yourself yet?"

"Small stuff, routine payoffs. But Torrance just unraveled a good bust, and I'm starting to think he's deeper than we figured. Give me all you can on him."

"Does he trust you?"

"I think so. I'm still the new boy on the block, the good-natured rube."

"I'll send you the files within the week. Have you met with Rachel lately?"

Alex hesitated. He hadn't even thought about Rachel for a

week. Especially after he had met Chicago. "No, I haven't had anything new for her. I'll call her tomorrow."

Alex hung up and leaned against the phone booth, stretching his calves. His bike rested against a cypress tree, the sun shining on its bronze paint. It was an older bike, heavy by today's standards, but it was Apollo's chariot to Alex. The $8000 hand-built masterpiece he kept for racing and his mountain bike had been donated to (or procured by) his younger sister and left behind in North Dakota. Alex had never really gotten into off-road biking; it was the smooth speed he craved, not dirt in his teeth.

He even had an old Schwinn, a mule of a bike, with a flat, round seat and coaster brakes that he rode now and then. He liked the sounds it made. This Bianchi, though, was his favorite. It was a faithful bike, fast and light but sturdy. It seemed to have adapted to him over the years. An injury had left his left leg stronger than his right (machete wounds are like that), and this uneven pedaling sometimes slipped the chain on his more sensitive racer. But the Bianchi accepted him and seemed to thrive with lopsided glory. He slipped his water bottle back in the holster, checked his brakes for dirt, squeezed the tires, and began the ride home.

By the time he got back to Miami, it was nearly dark. Alex had ridden over a hundred miles, and his whole body was vibrating. It was the feeling he craved: total depletion, his senses numbed by the concentration and exertion, an almost hallucinatory exhaustion. The ground felt rubbery under his feet and his hands were numb from the vibration of the road. The bicycle seemed light as a scarf as he lifted it to hang in the garage. He closed the garage door and peeled off his cycling gloves. Only then did he notice the truck parked in front of his house.

His eyes were dry and stinging. He had to blink and squint into the twilight before he saw that it was Chicago climbing out.

"I called you at the station, but you weren't there. You weren't

here either, so I finally just came and waited." Chicago slammed
the door of her truck and started talking as she crossed the lawn.
"We have to talk. I found things out . . ." She wasn't limping
anymore.

Alex brought her inside and unceremoniously strode to the
kitchen, where he drank three glasses of water. He was soaked
with sweat and the muscles in the back of his neck were starting
to ache.

"These two guys at the marina, George Tessely and—"

"Wait," he said firmly, interrupting Chicago's attempts to talk.
"I just rode a hundred miles. I need food, drink, a shower, and
maybe a half hour of *Mr. Rogers' Neighborhood*. If you let me
take a shower and make about eight sandwiches out of whatever
you can find while I'm in there, I will not only listen but I'll be
your slave for life."

Chapter 8

"Okay, this is what it is . . ." Chicago continued. They sat on the glider in the screened back porch eating sardine, tomato, and lima-bean sandwiches on pita bread and drinking Chimay Ale. The beer was dark and malty, brewed by monks in dark wool robes. You could almost chew it. Alex drank nothing that could come with ice, fruit, or sip straws; cheap whiskey and good beer made him happy.

". . . I'm cutting a gasket at the marina this morning when George Tessely comes in for air fills," Chicago went on. "He has this beautiful boat—a motor cruiser, one of those Super-Cobra-Zenith XR-T8O-Z-whatever kind of boats." She was clearly not up on makes and models of powerboats. "He bought it just two months ago, despite the fact that before this he'd always been just another average boat bum, running small fishing charters and an occasional salvage."

Alex picked up his third sandwich and forced himself to concentrate on her story. He was beginning to feel a sweet contentment. He was honestly tired and newly clean. The food and beer were soaking in. He would not have thought of putting lima beans inside a sandwich, or if he had, he probably would have thawed them first, but they did give it a certain textural flair. His muscles were relaxed, his cells no longer jangled, and here was an interesting woman for company, one who, he had now decided, was far more beautiful than Jane Goodall and Dian Fossey combined. If only she would forget about this shark conspiracy stuff.

"Umbi filled his scuba tanks," she continued, talking between bites. "And hustler that he is, he offered to hose down and scrub the decks for a few extra bucks. While Umbi's brushing the deck, he knocks a tarp aside—" Chicago paused, clearly for dramatic effect. "Tessely has shark suits with his scuba gear."

Alex waited. She looked at him expectantly.

"What's a shark suit?" he asked dumbly.

"Jesus Christ," she said, leaping off the seat. "Don't you get *National Geographic* in North Dakota? They had a whole spread on it! Valerie Taylor had to stuff mackerel up her arms to get the sharks to bite, but it was great footage. It's like a suit of chain mail. Sharks can't bite through it."

"Well, after your munching, it sounds like a pretty good idea."

"Damnit, Alex, I told you that was an aberration!" She paced across the little porch, hitting the wood frame in places for punctuation.

Alex sighed. He had never met anyone so adamant in defending something that had recently chomped a hole in her leg.

"But that's what Tessely said, too! Only, I know it's not true. For one thing, the suits cost thousands of dollars, and you don't just go down to K Mart and pick one up. They're hard to come by, and anyway, there's no reason to have one unless you're purposely diving in feeding frenzies with bait in your armpits! Sharks don't just take bites out of people," Chicago continued as she dropped back down beside him. She smelled sweet and crisp. There were aluminum shavings clinging to her T-shirt, like glitter. Why was that so sexy?

". . . That alone should tell you something strange is going on out there!" Alex still looked skeptical.

"Look," she continued. "I've been diving since I was ten years old. I've seen hundreds of sharks and never anything like that. There has never, *ever* been a documented incident of a shark attack on a submerged scuba diver! Dogs kill more people than sharks do! Hell, bees kill more people than sharks do! Sharks get surfers and the occasional snorkeler, spearfishermen with fresh catches, but not divers. This whole thing at Osprey was totally abnormal."

"Maybe Osprey Reef is some kind of international convention hall for sharks, a breeding ground or audition set for the next *Jaws*. Maybe Tessely just knew that and bought the suit because he wanted to dive at Osprey."

"But that's it! There's no reason to dive at Osprey. They used to blow up missles there; everything's wrecked. I only went for tropical fish and Tessely doesn't have a collector's license."

"Well, if that's the case, I could certainly write him a ticket."

Chicago leapt up again and stared at him, her pale eyes icy with a fury he had seen before. Alex groaned; even if she didn't outright hit him, there didn't seem to be much chance she was going to curl up in his arms right now and listen to the tree frogs peep.

"For a fucking detective, you couldn't find your way out of Chutes and Ladders! Just think about it!" Another switch; she softened, perched on the edge of the glider, and leaned toward him.

"Listen, I know you're tired, but just think about this. George Tessely, general slackard, suddenly comes into a lot of money and buys an expensive boat. George Tessely, who has never been much of a scuba diver—I know, because I do most of the air fills— suddenly is so passionate about the sport that he turns down an opportunity for a good fishing charter last Friday in order to go diving with his buddy Eli Turner, who has also been flashing big bucks around." She paused to let that sink in. It was working.

"Last Friday?" She nodded. "And you were bitten on a Friday, the week before?"

"Yes!"

"Maybe they're Catholic sharks and they have to eat people on Fridays." He ducked as Chicago swung at him. "Okay, okay, I'll be serious." He stretched his legs out and rested his head on the back of the cushion, noticed a mud-wasp nest starting in a corner of the porch ceiling. He found himself growing interested in spite of his better logic.

"Okay." He tried to sound like a detective. "They have reason to dive at Osprey Reef, reason to expect sharks there. And somehow enough profit out of it all that they'll spend thousands of dollars on protective suits."

"Bingo, you win the bedroom suite, the microwave, and the patio furniture."

"Is there any reason there would be so many sharks at Osprey Reef?"

"I'm not sure—they still don't know much about shark behavior. But the site is unusual, that deep trench. They found a place off North Carolina recently that might be a mating ground. Look, I'll show you." She dug around in her shoulder bag, pulled out some charts, and spread them out on Alex's lap, smoothing the paper so it lay flat. Alex smiled at her hands moving so boldly across his lap.

"You missed a few wrinkles."

"Osprey Reef is here,"—she ignored the remark and traced a line with her finger—"right on the edge of the offshore plateau. See how this ridge goes? All along this line there's a drop off of thirty feet, then another here, and here, like steps. That's typical for the coast along here, but Osprey sticks up off the second plateau, and there's a trench to the seaward edge. Then all over here"—she pointed to little X's and triangles on the chart—"are reef fragments, or atolls. The place is a bitch to navigate around.

Nobody likes to get boats near there. There are two big freighter wrecks that I know of, possibly more."

"Could it be something valuable in the shipwrecks? Sunken treasure?"

Chicago frowned. "I thought of that. I already checked. The *D'Angelou* went down around here. She was running almost empty, had off-loaded in Miami the day before a labor strike, and was just hanging out waiting. The *Aspen* is there." She pointed and a shiver ran up Alex's spine. "It had general cargo but was pretty well salvaged. She's only in eighty to ninety feet."

"There could always have been something—gold, jewels."

"Yeah, but if you find diamonds, you talk about it. If you find any kind of treasure, you can claim salvage rights. And why not go out every day? Why only once a week? Once Umbi and I started thinking about it, we realized that Tessely hasn't taken a charter on a Friday for months. He just goes diving with Eli."

"Friday!" Suddenly, Alex had the kind of hunch that clanged right up his spine like one of those carnival strength-meters.

"What do you know about the Redondo fish co-op?"

Chicago looked puzzled and shrugged. "Not much. It's a small operation, buys mostly from the last few small independent fishermen, specialty stuff I think. A Spanish woman started it, Gloria something. A couple of years ago, when Miami began to boom and all these fancy restaurants came in, she got the idea to supply them."

"Who does she buy from?"

"Everyone, really. I know some guys who go out just for Redondo, but anyone with extra-big lobsters or a good fresh catch can get a better price there. Someone may sell most of his catch to the big packers but save the choicest stuff for Redondo. The packers get pissed, but she's been pretty successful. What are you thinking?"

"Nothing yet, but the name was dropped at a little party last week."

Chicago's eyes brightened. "Eli Turner used to drive delivery trucks for Redondo. He may still." Alex looked back over the charts. Chicago noticed that he seemed to know how to read nautical charts pretty well for a farm boy. He didn't look at the key or ask her about any of the symbols.

"The ships, they're metal-hulled?"

"Yeah." Chicago looked at him. "Yeah, you could find them on sonar. You could find the trench, too."

"Can you take me there?"

She looked surprised. "Do you dive?"

"Ah, no, but you're an instructor, aren't you? You can teach me. I'm a good swimmer. I was a lifeguard once. Are you busy tomorrow?" He immediately wished he had used more tact. She probably wasn't so eager to return to the site of a shark attack.

If Chicago was bothered by the thought, she didn't show it. "Scuba's easy, but it takes more than one day to learn."

"I just want to have a look around. I can swim and I can breathe. What more is there?"

Chicago laughed. "I can take you through the basics, and if you do okay, we'll do the dive. But not tomorrow."

Alex looked over the chart again.

"This"—Alex pointed to the chart, but looked her in the eye, with a burning interest she had not expected—"is a shipping lane."

The next thing she did not expect was Alex's hands around the back of her head, grabbing double handfuls of her hair and pulling her into a kiss that was more than the exuberant rejoicing of partners against crime.

He felt her lips soft for a moment, then she sprang away. For a second, she looked truly surprised, unguarded, and maybe about to cry, then her eyes narrowed.

"Hey, I'm sorry," Alex quickly offered. "Isn't that what they do by now in the cop shows?" he added lightly.

"This ain't no goddamn cop show." She snatched up her charts and slammed out the door.

Chapter 9

Tuesday morning it rained. Chief Torrance hung up the phone and stared gloomily out at the gray. Now he had to think of a whole new plan. He sighed and tossed his golf glove onto the chair, pulled his shoes out of the bag, and reinserted the stretchers. Better put this away somewhere safe, he thought as he pulled out the tube of sunscreen lotion. His wife never went out into the sun and was unlikely ever to touch it, but he wanted to be safe.

For the tube was filled not with sunblock (SPF 15 with aloe and lanolin) but with transdermal nitroglycerin cream. He had learned about the cream when his father was recovering from a heart attack. In the hospital, the cream was smeared on a little patch and left on the patient's chest. The drug was slowly absorbed through the skin and it lowered blood pressure. At the time, it had been just another marvel of medical technology. Only later had it occurred to Torrance what a good murder weapon it might be.

Judge Selby burned easily and hated hats. His bald head needed protection from the strong Florida sun that was supposed to be burning down on their golf game today. The judge had a heart condition anyway. He was currently leading his friends and colleagues in the bypass tally with a double. Torrance knew that

Selby took nitro pills for angina, so this wouldn't look at all suspicious. A few applications would have done the trick. It would, according to Torrance's consultant, look like a stroke.

But now it was foggy and wet and he had to think of something else, and soon. Another try at golf was out. It had taken weeks to find time for today's game in the judge's busy schedule. No, he would just have to start plan B.

"I need shipping registers for all cruise lines running out of Miami, particularly anything on a weekly turnaround coming in on Friday mornings; coast guard navigational updates; and salvage reports on all shipwrecks in the area of Osprey Reef. Got that?" Alex leaned impatiently toward the speaker phone.

"I can have the files on Tessely and Turner within the hour, sir. The rest is going to take time."

"Soon, please. I need it yesterday. Thank you."

"Assertive today, aren't we?" Wonton teased. "What makes you think it's a cruise ship?" He was interested in the theory but surprised by Alex's newfound zeal in a dead case.

"Think about it," Alex replied. "It looks like an amateur operation. We have small, regular amounts coming in on a regular schedule. Six months now; a few kilos a week coming in through Reggi's fish market, always on Friday. Now I've got two boat guys, Tessely and Turner, into sudden big money and diving every Friday morning on a certain spot adjacent to a shipping lane. One of them drives trucks for the Redondo fish co-op."

"Sounds good so far," Wonton admitted, his interest growing.

"From what I've found on Tessely, he doesn't have the connections to any big suppliers. He's not that bright or that brave. But he could easily have a friend on a cruise ship or freighter, someone who makes regular runs to the Caribbean and might make a few friends there. Someone who could make connections and do the small drops."

Alex paused and shuffled through a few papers. "And finally, did you look at the lab reports on the coke we seized in the fish market bust? It's pure as Mother Teresa. Ninety percent or so. They aren't even cutting it."

"Just want it in and out, huh? Hot potatoes?"

"Amateurs."

"So someone drops the snow on Osprey Reef, and Tessely and Turner go out for a little dive and happen to bring back a few k's. Nice treasure hunt. So let's just go down to the dock this Friday when they come in and reel them in."

Restless, Alex got up and paced across the small office. The rubber plant was looking peaked, so he gave it the rest of his coffee. It had started to put out new leaves. Maybe after all those years of solicitous care that had led to its demise, Alex had found the secret—benign neglect and black coffee.

"But, officer," Alex mimicked. "We just happened to find it lying on the bottom. We have no idea where it came from. . . . C'mon, Wonton, your menu's missing the entrees."

"So we stake them out."

"Underwater? Right. You hide behind a sea fan and I'll wear an octopus on my head."

"Okay, okay. So we'll work on it. Great ideas take a little time. I'll talk to Barnes—she's good at planning these things. You think they deal directly with Reggi?"

"I don't know. We don't know where the whole thing started. Could be Tessely, could be Morales, could be whoever is supplying on the other end."

"Could be we need to talk to Morales some more. If he's squealing on the big guys, he won't mind tossing us these pests. The department's always eager for a good little publicity bust—this could be just the thing."

"Can you talk to him?" Alex looked doubtful.

"He's in a safe house, but the captain can arrange it. I'll get on it." Wonton stood up. He was really quite graceful for someone his size, but when he stood next to things like chairs or bicycles, he looked crushing.

"Do you want to get some lunch first?"

"Can't," Alex replied, shuddering a little at the notion of a "publicity bust" coming from Wonton, who he had respected as someone with at least a hint of anarchy. But then maybe I don't know you so well after all, he thought. "I've got an appointment."

Chapter 10

"God, Alex, where have you been these days! I'm going nuts down here playing junior law clerk. A girl can only take so much of loafers and navy suits."

Rachel Brannet had unpinned her legal bun and now tossed her blond hair in a flirtatious gesture that Alex recognized but was no longer tempted by. They had enjoyed a brief affair shortly after meeting on this case. It wasn't exactly in the lines of FBI undercover policy, but since they were working in separate areas, with little contact otherwise, it wasn't that far out of line either. And by now Alex had little respect for agency lines anyway.

He had, however, finally used this excuse to ease out of the relationship. Things were fine; they got along well. Rachel was just over thirty, amicably divorced, and seemed content with their superficial involvement. Sex was fun, and since they were both new to Miami, it was a convenient friendship. It would not seem unusual for a cop to date a law clerk, so there was no threat to their covers.

It was just . . . something. Alex couldn't define it. After a couple of months he simply began to feel restless, as if he were going through the same thing again. He liked Rachel. She was smart and attractive and whatever women are when they're too old to be bubbly but still make you feel light when they're around. Her hair was almost naturally blond and her makeup was never extreme, though Alex preferred the subdued look she wore now.

She's pretty, he found himself thinking now, in a usual sort of way; pretty like the women in TV ads for after-shave.

"So how've you been?"

"Fine. It's been busy at the precinct. We're working on a drug case."

"You're involved as a real cop on a real case?"

"I am a real cop, aren't I?"

"I don't know. You may not even have the power to arrest someone in Miami—unless it's a federal statute."

"It's something that grew out of the Morales bust."

"Morales—he's the guy Selby let go a couple of weeks ago?"

Alex nodded and filled Rachel in on the details of the fish market bust and the subsequent developments with Tessely and Turner. He left out Chicago.

"So you're going after them now?"

"Yeah, maybe. We just got a few possible leads." There was a pause. Rachel was never very good with pauses. To her they were aneurysms in the conversation and she feared their collapse.

"So I guess since this joint is miles out of the way and everyone is speaking either Yiddish or Spanish, you want to discuss the investigation."

Alex laughed.

"Braddock sent me files for you."

"I'll trade you." Alex offered her the stack he had brought and took the new ones. They turned their attention to the real case.

"We have good evidence on everyone marked in yellow, but these guys,"—Alex reached over and flipped a few pages—"I think, are the major ones. Graft, extortion, tampering with evidence, the regular stuff. I'm not sure I'll be let in deep enough there. We may have to rely on pressure and plea bargains from the peons."

"What about Captain Torrance?"

"He's an enigma. I'm sure he's dirty, but there's nothing to tie him to Roscoe or Peterson or any of the others. I can't get a handle on it. Does Selby ever mention him?"

"They were supposed to play golf today but called the game because of the weather. I personally don't see the fat judge hitting the ball far enough to have fog be a problem, but they don't really socialize beyond golf and community fund-raisers."

"Have you talked to headquarters lately?"

"No, but Donovan and Morris have. Alex, I think there's some pressure to get this wrapped up. Donovan went to Washington last weekend. It seems there's some political things going on. State congressional elections are coming up in Florida, and the Republican administration would like the chance to make the current Democrats look bad."

"Are we investigating politicos in this thing, too?"

"No. Political corruption isn't news," she joked. "No, this is more guilt by association. How-could-you have-run-a-county-and-not-known-what-was-going-on sort of thing."

"I'm not rushing this thing. Damn bureaucrats and politicians. I want something hard on Torrance. How does the judge look?"

Rachel shrugged. "I have circumstantial evidence—conflict of interest, questionable tax returns, dubious acquittals, and technicality releases. There are dozens of those. I have some evidence of bribery, but nothing airtight. Selby's a gambler. There's talk that he hasn't been hitting many winners lately."

"What does he bet on?"

"Vertabrates."

"What would it take to nail him down?"

"A wiretap of him saying, 'Why, yes, Señor Kalispel, just give me one hundred thousand dollars and your man who has smuggled tons of cocaine will go home today.' It might help if he snorts a couple of lines real loud, too," she added sarcastically.

"Is Selby using?"

"I don't think so. He doesn't act like it. It's not his style. Selby's strictly a martini man. And he has a heart condition. I think his only drug is money."

They ran over the rest of the new material, comparing notes and deciding what direction to take now, then Rachel had to leave. Alex kissed her lightly and tucked the files back into the folder. As soon as he got outside, though, he stopped, opened them again, and scanned the suspect list quickly for Detective Frank Baxter. No highlights.

Chapter 11

"You know the best thing about being rich, Eli?" Tessely leaned back against the glove-soft leather, his eyes fixed on the well-spangled figures of the two women as they wove their way through the crowd to the powder room. "You just can't be too rude." And to illustrate his point, he snapped his fingers at a passing waiter and demanded a fresh bottle of champagne.

"This one's starting to sweat!" he barked. "And here we got a regular table in the top club, and broads who would go out and have our names tattooed across their foreheads if we asked. It's a great life, a good life," he declared as he downed the rest of his champagne.

George Tessely still considered champagne somewhere between soda pop and Kool-Aid, but he ordered it for effect. Eli Turner, however, had developed a real taste for the stuff and was at the moment fairly drunk. Despite their new clothes and attitude of wealth, the two men still looked out of place among the beautiful people in the nightclub. Both were rough-skinned and tanned in the uneven way that told of labor outdoors instead of afternoons in the tanning booth. It was uniquely a waterman's tan, with bronzed forearms and subtle shading on the underside of cheekbone and jaw from reflections off the water.

Tessely stood about five feet seven, but his build gave the impression of height. Years of shrimping and lobstering had given him a solid chest and heavily muscled arms. Years of beer drinking had given him a belly, but it too was solid, shored up by still decent abdominal muscles, so it protruded in a smooth, squarish plane from chest to belt. When he lay down, it looked rather like a mesa. He still had a thick head of curly hair, dirty-blond streaked with gray, which, at fifty-two, made him feel particularly virile.

The two men were actually the same height, but Eli Turner seemed smaller. He had a wiry build, cobbled over with tight, round muscles. There was a sharp, bristly quality about him. His features were pointed, his eyes permanently squinted, his hair kinky and thin. He had spent most of his life drifting from job to job—deckhand, fisherman, engine-room worker. During occasional lapses into sobriety and industry he had managed to acquire his captain's license and had piloted boats, usually to the brink of catastrophe.

Turner didn't talk much, especially when he was drinking. It usually got him in trouble, and besides, he was always snagging his tongue. Most of the teeth that had survived his lifelong poor oral hygiene had been knocked out in brawls. Now that he was rich, he was in the process of having them all capped with gold, and each new restoration meant learning to navigate words all over again.

"Good evening, gentlemen." Two men were standing in front of their table. They were well dressed and sober. They didn't look like they were soliciting for the Salvation Army. "While your ladies are away, we thought we might have a discussion." The two men slid into the booth on either side of Tessely and Turner. One was a small, solid black man as broad as he was tall. You could sit a librarian on each of his shoulders and still have room for the narrower volumes of *Encyclopaedia Britannica.* He wore a row of gold rings that fringed the entire rim of one ear. The other man was tall and graceful, with long hands and oiled-down hair.

"A business discussion," the tall man explained. "We represent a certain party who is in the same line of work as you gentlemen."

"Oh yeah?" Tessely feigned friendly interest. "Well, who's that? You know, I know most of the charter captains—we're a close bunch . . ."

"That's not the line of work I'm referring to. Please don't try to be glib, Mr. Tessely, it doesn't become you and you're not very good at it." The man lifted the champagne bottle from its bucket and gave a little amused snort at the label. "Dom Perignon. A certain lack of sophistication, wouldn't you say, Mr. Moray?"

The black man said nothing. He sat like a stone. The only motion was the pulsing of enlarged blood vessels stretched across his massive biceps. This guy hadn't heard all the nasty news about steroids. He made Ben Johnson look like Don Knotts. "It's trite; it positively screams nouveau riche," the tall man continued. "Try a Roederer Cristal next time, Mr. Tessely, or a Bollinger RD. You can have them leave the price tag on if your guests are too ignorant to recognize excellence."

"Look, whoever you are, you're starting to bother me," Tessely broke in with his best waterfront swagger.

"Just now?" The tall man feigned disappointment. "I must be losing my touch. I'm usually annoying the moment I sit down."

"What do you want anyhow, buddy?" Eli slurred.

"Now, that's a quality I admire—directness. Let me be direct then. You may call me Mr. Soulange. My employer wishes me first of all to congratulate you on the cleverness of your enterprise. It's a sweet little operation—a little play-schoolish, perhaps, but not bad for amateurs. Unfortunately, there are certain realities of this business you have been overlooking." Soulange brushed the ash from his cigarette into Tessely's champagne. "To put it simply, the Miami board of unofficial trade isn't happy with you butting in."

"I don't know what you're talking about," Tessely protested, but the tremor in his voice betrayed him.

"Then perhaps you better take notes and look up the big words in the dictionary. We have no use for small-time independent operators." He leaned back to let this sink in then, turning with a smile that came out like fingernails on a chalkboard, made his offer.

"You, sir, have no business in our business. We own the cocaine routes, and we have exclusive rights to a certain sector of this city. We are, however, willing to consider keeping you on as we enlarge your enterprise."

"Wait a minute! You—you can't do that!"

"Mr. Tessely, fifty feet away on that balcony by the potted fern, at an angle of approximately thirty degrees, the barrel of an Intratec 9mm with silencer is aimed at your head. I can do anything I want."

Eli blinked and looked from one man to another. He felt sick. He made a vow then and there to quit this champagne shit and stick to beer. He never felt this way from beer.

Tessely swallowed and narrowed his eyes. He was a pragmatic man, a man who, like all the ordinary men who have acquiesced to all the ordinary acts of horror in the world, took some pride in his ability to know when his back was against the wall and just how low to stoop to get himself free.

"All right, what's the deal?"

"Well done," the man crooned. "It's so nice to avoid upsetting Mr. Moray. Here's the arrangement. You increase your supply— let's go for double right now—and we take care of distribution. The fish thing was cute, but there's really no need for all that subterfuge. You're transporting in scuba tanks, right? Once you bring the tanks in, you need only to unload the merchandise and deliver it to a location we will arrange. This fish co-op place may even continue to serve."

Tessely shook his head impatiently. Already he was feeling proud and important again, flattered in fact, and determined to hold on to some control.

"First of all, Redondo isn't involved. Eli just drives their trucks. It's owned by this old Cuban bitch, Bible in one hand, her old man's balls in the other. Second, I can't increase supply. I've got one guy who knows one guy. Even if there were more to be had, I don't think he could handle it."

"We can handle it, Mr. Tessely. The *Seastar* is not the only ship plying the waters between Miami and the Caribbean, and your brother the boiler man is not the only person capable of tossing scuba tanks over the side." The tall man nodded to Mr. Moray, who gave his biceps one last flex as he rose from the table.

"The details will take care of themselves—it was your cooperation we wanted to establish tonight. I'm so glad to have made your acquaintance. Good night, gentlemen. And remember about the champagne. Would you like me to write it down for you?"

Chapter 12

"This is your regulator." Chicago held up the apparatus, a combination of black hoses and clunky metal parts. "This part is called the first stage." She screwed it onto the valve of the scuba tank. "The first stage takes the air down from the high pressure inside the tank to about a hundred psi. This part is the second stage." It was a fist-size metal piece with a clear silicone mouthpiece. She handed it to Alex and turned the tank valve so air flowed into the hoses, stiffening them slightly. "Second stage delivers the air at ambient pressure; that means it adjusts to whatever the water pressure around you is, so it's never hard to breathe. Try it." They were in a little sheltered bay south of the city, preparing for Alex's dive on Osprey Reef. Alex put the regulator in his mouth and took a few breaths.

"Feels like normal."

"It is normal."

"What about this one?" Alex held up the second mouthpiece, identical except for its bright orange casing and orange hose.

"It's an octopus, a backup—in case you have an asshole buddy who runs out of air or something. Now, *you* never run out of air." She picked up the gauge, also attached by a hose to the first stage. "That's what this is for. You read the dial, you know how much air you have. And the reg never cuts off—that's all *Sea Hunt* dramatic bullshit." Alex smiled. Her teaching style was a mix of soft reassurance and her usual barbs. "If it does fuck up, which it almost never does, it doesn't stop your air. It free-flows, gives it to you constantly."

"Oh, mon, but you don't need no air when the shark bite your heads off," Umbi interjected from the shade of a palm tree, where he lay watching the lesson.

"Umbi, why don't you go lick barnacles off my bottom."

"Them sharks are melting butter right now to dip you in 'fore they eat you up."

Chicago ignored him and turned back to the lesson. "Now, this is your B.C., or buoyancy compensator—"

"Or big chunk outta you . . ." More mumblings from the palm tree.

"It's what makes diving possible for the timid masses."

"Yeah, that's me!" Alex admitted cheerfully as he looked it over. It was a simple thing, an inflatable orange vest with buckles in the front. There was a fat accordianlike hose with a metal fitting sprouting from the shoulder. Chicago attached the last hose from the scuba tank to the fitting on the B.C.

"Hit this button"—she squeezed a button on the B.C. hose with her thumb—"and air from the tank goes in. Hit this one"— she held the hose up and hit another button on the bottom— "and the air goes out. Keep it full on the surface and you float. Let some air out and you start to sink."

"It's like a life jacket."

"Sort of, but it's more. It keeps your weight adjusted while you're underwater. It has to do with depth and pressure and expansion of gasses and stuff like that, but you learn all that in the full PADI open-water-certification program." She laughed. "That's the word from our sponsor to get you to sign up for the whole course and really learn this stuff. Anyway, the B.C. adjusts your buoyancy. But don't you go messing with it today. I'll adjust you if you need it. Shouldn't need it much anyway, we're not going very deep."

"Naw, don't need to go very deep. Sharks be glad to swim up to where you be." Chicago pitched a rock at the tree or at Umbi, Alex wasn't sure which. It smacked the trunk a few inches above his head.

"Here's a weight belt." She stepped back and looked him over as if appraising a horse. "What do you weigh, one seventy, one eighty?"

"Don't I have to give you a penny to guess that?"

"But you're pretty dense," she continued, ignoring his humor. "With no wet suit, let's try four pounds."

Finally, Chicago and Alex put the equipment on and waded out into the bay.

"And what's the most important rule of scuba diving?" she asked again.

"Always keep breathing, never hold my breath."

"Good. Let's do it."

They dropped to their knees in the shallow water. She showed him how to clear water from his mask, how to dip his shoulder and sweep with one arm to find his regulator if it should come out of his mouth, and how to find her octopus in case he ran out of air. She explained how to pinch his nose and gently blow to equalize the pressure in his ears during descent. They swam around the shallow lagoon for a few minutes until she was convinced that he was comfortable.

"Well, that's it." Chicago smiled when they surfaced. "You did great, really good. You learn fast. I guess we can go," she offered. Alex noted the slight hint of apprehension in her voice. He had borrowed a boat from the station. She fussed about arranging the gear, then looked over toward Umbi, who appeared to be asleep under his tree.

"Hey, fish breath! C'mon, let's go!"

Humberto pulled his lanky body off the sand and waded into the bay toward the boat, shaking his head and muttering his objections. In a few minutes they were on their way to Osprey Reef. It was a calm day, but there was a little surface chop. The trip took forty-five minutes. As they neared the reef, Umbi slowed the throttle, shaded his eyes, and scanned the turquoise water that marked the edge of the reef. He thought for only a minute, then steered them to a spot.

"Maybe a little further south," Chicago directed, gazing down into the water.

"This the place. I know. I promise you this right where we were."

"It looks fine to me," Alex offered. While he wasn't exactly reeling, he was seasick enough that the last place he wanted to be was bobbing around on the surface.

"Well, I think we could scope it out better first. I mean, you want to see the whole area, don't you?"

"Actually, I'd like to get in the water," Alex said.

Umbi gave an exaggerated sigh. "What you want to drive around for? The parking lot's empty. This place good as any other. See, the wreck right over there. I bet you we right on top of our anchor . . ."

"Who's fucking this monkey!" Chicago snapped. "I don't think this is the place. And I want to check out the atolls."

"Can't we do that better snorkeling?" Alex pointed out, firmer this time but with the sweat starting to show and an uneasiness in his stomach. There was a silent standoff in the little boat. The afternoon sun glared off the water.

"Hoo, boy, I think we in need of one of them Phil Donahue Show psychology people. Why don't you guys just admit yourselves? Here the facts." He pointed at Chicago. "You scared of the sharks, as you damn should be, and you"—he pointed at Alex—

"is seasick. So why don' we all give it up and go home. You want to see some underwater scenics, we can watch Jacques Cousteau."

"Shit." Chicago snatched up her weight belt and began to fumble with the buckle.

"Hey," Alex said gently. "You know, he's right. I am seasick."

"Well, I'm damn well not scared!" But she was embarrassed to feel her eyes growing wet. "Let's just do this." They dropped the anchor. She helped Alex on with his gear, got her own on, and showed him how to do a back roll off the side.

Once in, her sense of professionalism overcame her fear. Having a novice to watch out for absorbed her attention. She stayed close and watched Alex carefully. Would he choke and panic the first time he got a little water in his mask? Would he get spooked by something, chase off after big fish, drop his weight belt, or—the biggest nightmare—hold his breath and bolt to the top? In all her years of teaching, and with all the panicked students she had successfully intercepted, this could still get her heart pounding. It didn't take much; bolting up a mere ten feet with lungs full of compressed air could cause a fatal embolism. Alex seemed comfortable, and Chicago began to relax.

The dive was uneventful. They saw lots of dead coral and only one small shark, which swam placidly below them, accompanied by various unworried smaller fish. The only thing out of the ordinary was the amount of trash in the area. She had been too busy looking for fish the first time to notice it. They swam over rusted oil cans, plastic bottles, and the other sad debris of an overtrashed ocean. They swam over the wrecked freighters, between the atolls, and out to the edge of the reef, where the wall dropped away into deep water.

Chicago found the moray's hole and spied the nose of the green eel poking out of a hole. She motioned to Alex to come see. They swam close and watched it watch them. She should have thought to bring some food and start taming it. Chicago liked eels and knew that the vicious-looking snapping motions they made with their mouths was just the way they breathed.

Once they got used to contact, they could be almost friendly. She liked to pet them; the skin was smooth and velvety. She made a mental note to call the Disney World Living Seas director and see if they were still looking for a moray. Alex hovered and watched, fascinated.

Umbi waited in the boat alone. More alone than Chicago and Alex could ever have imagined. There were a few moments two weeks ago, after the attack, while he and Chicago were floating in terrified isolation, when it seemed all his questions might finally have been resolved. At that moment, he had fully expected to be killed and eaten by the sharks and had found in that thought a powerful, sweet relief. There are things more painful than death.

Why had he survived? Why was it the other boat and not his that sank that night? They had left Haiti with two small boats, both overloaded with refugees. There were eight families, in little fishing boats belonging to his father and brother Emilio. The sea was rough, and just after noon on the second day out, a wave swamped Emilio's boat. It began to sink. His father had turned their boat to sail to their aid, but an argument broke out.

"There is no room! We can't take them in! You will drown us all!"

His father's boat was sturdier, but it was built for a dozen and already carrying twenty-eight. The women screamed, some with pleas for their drowning friends, some with threats. "My children are here! You won't kill us all twice over!" Umbi was thirteen. He and his brother Duvy tried to aid their father, but another man struck them down and took the rudder.

In the water, some of the people clung to the overturned hull and some began to swim toward their boat. Some men threw out lines; others struck these men and tried to cut the lines free. One pulled out a knife and stabbed Duvy, who was reaching for Emilio. Umbi remembered the fighting and, always, the silent faces in the darkening sea. Their cries were lost in the waves.

The fighting on his wretched boat stopped suddenly as sharks appeared. As if his ears had been covered and now suddenly were open, Umbi heard the screams. The sharks' bodies were sleek and hard as iron. The water began to redden with blood. They cut the surface, thrashing and snapping for a furious eternity. All afternoon the frenzy went on. A large ship passed in the distance and some of the women waved scarves, but it was a hopeless, pathetic gesture. The afternoon sun was hot and the smell of blood was nauseating. The refugees soon fell into silence, no one sailing or steering, as the sun set and the water grew finally calm.

Chicago and Alex broke the surface right beside the boat.

"Hey, Umbi!" she called. There was no response. "Hey, banana butt, you sleeping?" Chicago banged on the hull. "We found the anchor. C'mon—wake up and give us a hand." Umbi appeared by the stern, looking somber and distracted. He reached over and took the anchor.

"So there, so you see it, right? It's been cut!" Chicago was waving the end of the anchor line under Alex's nose. "It's been cut, like I said!" Even after a couple of weeks underwater, the end of the rope appeared to be cleanly cut, not frayed and snapped. They handed up their gear and climbed into the boat. "So admit it, squid brain," she insisted. "Those guys cut our anchor line!"

"Well, damn," Alex declared with a trace of sarcasm. "I'll go right in and issue a warrant for their arrest. This is certainly convincing evidence."

Umbi ignored the banter, started the motor, and began to pull up the anchor. Chicago noticed his mood. She went forward to give him a hand. "Are you okay?" she asked gently.

Umbi nodded and sniffed. "I just developed a severe allergy to this location," he lied, then ducked his head, and the issue.

Chapter 13

While Alex was diving on Osprey Reef, Wonton waited on a bench on the far north end of Miami Beach drinking a bottle of red Nehi and waiting for Morales. He glanced at his watch. Barnes was to have picked up Morales at two; they should have been here by now. He stood and stretched. It was a nice section of beach; maybe he ought to bring Ellen and Dusty out here. They never went to the beach anymore. He remembered the three of them coming often once—how much equipment it required to take a baby to the beach! Blankets and umbrellas and a portable bed with a fly screen so that Dusty wouldn't be bit. But no—that wasn't right exactly; that wasn't Dusty. That was Joey, his first child. That was ten years ago, when Joseph had been small and still manageable.

He heard his name, turned, and saw Barnes walking toward him. She carried her shoes and slipped awkwardly in the sand. She had a bad-news look on her face. Wonton glanced past her and saw a uniformed officer waiting by the car alone.

"Where's Morales?" he asked, aware something had gone wrong.

She shook her head. "Someone shot him. He's dead." She brushed back hairs that were sticking to her damp forehead. "Right outside the safe house as we were walking him to the car."

"Christ, Missy, are you okay?"

"Yeah, yeah, I'm fine. A little shaken," she added. "It was a good shot. Sounded like a handgun, a .38 maybe, so it couldn't have been too far away. We've got people all over the place."

"Where's Torrance? Does he know?"

"He's at the house. He was one of the first ones there. They've got ballistics there, homicide, everybody." She waved her hand in an impatient gesture, then shaded her eyes from the sun, glanced up and down the beach.

"Shit." Wonton sighed.

"Screw much up?"

Wonton shrugged. "Not for our little bust, I guess. It would have been nice if we could've got something on Tessely and Turner, but that's not such a big deal. If he was really going to rat on Kalispel, we're back to nowhere again. It was starting to look a little too easy."

Chicago steered the borrowed boat up to the dock, and Umbi jumped out to tie them up. Alex climbed out and Chicago handed him the empty scuba tanks. "Just set them over there by the compressor," she told him. "I've got to start filling those others." She watched as Alex carried the tanks toward the shed. She liked the set of his shoulders, the long muscles in his back, the ease of his strength, the way he walked on the outside of his heels, with a little rolling motion. There was a leonine quality about him that aroused her. He wore faded gym shorts and a T-shirt so old it had started disintegrating in little holes across the back. Very sexy.

She felt suddenly hot and turned away to off-load the rest of the equipment. Passion had been long buried; she had not expected it to rekindle so suddenly or strongly, and not just by this ordinary scene. Umbi had already started setting the empty tanks in the water bath to be filled. Chicago climbed out and ducked inside, began to pull the compressor hoses off their hooks.

"Do you have to do that right now?" Alex stood at the doorway of the shed. She flipped the compressor switch. He had to shout to be heard over the noise. "I thought we could get a late lunch."

Chicago just shook her head and began screwing the fill hoses on the tanks. She wanted him to go. She felt suddenly strange, flushed and stupid.

"I have to get this done," she shouted. "I—ah, I promised to have some of these ready by six."

"I can fill 'em," Umbi offered. She shot him a look. He ignored it. "Ain't that many. Show me which need to be out first."

"The compressor's been acting funny. I think I better stick around." As she went to attach the last tank, she noticed the valve was loose in her hand. She bent to examine it and saw that the area around the valve was corroded and pitted. "Who the hell is diving with this?" she asked crossly, pulling the tank out of the rack and carrying it to the better light outside. Alex stepped back but did not move entirely to let her past. She had to slip by him close enough to feel the heat of his body.

"It's a mess. I can't fill this." Alex leaned over close to look at the tank. She stepped back and straightened, moved back a few steps.

"Looks like it's been underwater a month." She rolled the tank to each side looking for I.D. but found nothing.

"Umbi, whose tank is this? It's a steel seventy-two. It was with those other four—the blue eighties on that end."

Umbi looked at the row of tanks she was pointing to, then at the corroded one. "They all ones George Tessely bring in this morning."

She and Alex looked at each other meaningfully.

Chapter 14

Dominic Kalispel was sitting in front of his mirror examining the still-obvious results of his hair transplant. The hair was growing, and if he combed it straight back with enough gel, it didn't look so bad. Some men are meant to be bald, he thought, and I'm not one of them. He tried to tell himself it was an unreasonable embarrassment. Wasn't he still handsome and tan, with a solid phsyique? True, it had been getting a little extra solid around the belt these past few years, but a big man should look like a big man.

He smoothed the hair back carefully. He hadn't been out on his yacht for six months, simply to avoid the wind. He had never thought of himself as a vain man. It wasn't until that photo—that disgusting photographer who had snapped him from a balcony as he was leaving the DeAngelinis' party—showing the recent transplant like plugs of sod on his scalp that he had grown so sensitive. It had appeared in all the papers. Did the asshole know how lucky he was to have gotten away simply with having his studio blown up?

There was a knock on his door, and Soulange entered. "Mr. Kalispel sir, we just found out. Morales has been shot."

"Shot?"

"Killed, sir."

"Really?"

"Just a little while ago, sir."

"Was it us?"

"No, sir."

"Should it have been? I don't really remember." Kalispel paused as if in thought.

Soulange didn't interrupt. He had worked for Kalispel for six years, knew him as well as anyone could, but he could still never quite know when he was toying with you. It was possible that Kalispel had ordered Morales's execution through someone else, for some mind game or test of Soulange's acumen within the organization. He had done that before. It was also possible that he hadn't ordered it at all or had expected Soulange to take care of it. He knew the best tactic was to let Kalispel continue until he dropped his clue.

"He was the weasly one picked up in that fish market thing?" Kalispel continued. He ended all his sentences with a rising inflection.

"It is a nice development. He could have been a nuisance," Soulange offered.

"Hm," Kalispel mused. "Perhaps. Though if you think about it, Soulange, that whole thing has seemed a little strange from the start."

"How do you mean, sir?"

"Possession of four k's is hardly a big deal. That's all they caught him with, you know. Have you thought about that? Surely Mr. Morales has—had—a lawyer adroit enough to get him off without the risk involved in turning snitch."

"I could talk to our connection, sir. Find out what the police may be up to."

"Let it rest for the moment. If there's anything important, I'm sure we'll be told."

* * *

Alex spread the computer printouts over his desk. The pages were marked with different colors highlighting facts that might somehow tie in and show up some answers. Shipping routes, ports of call, files on the captains and crews of dozens of ships that sailed regular routes to the Caribbean. He was focusing on ships that docked in Miami, although there was no way to tell. It could as easily be a vessel out of anywhere on the East Coast. He just figured Turner and Tessely would be more likely to know someone on a local ship. It was dull stuff, but the dive that afternoon had left him with a lot of energy.

There were two memos on his desk when he arrived. One was from Barnes. "Redondo looks clean; Gloria Estebe cooperative. Confirmed Eli Turner sometimes drives for them, lots of deliveries on Fridays. Talk to you more A.M."

The other was from Wonton. "Going fishing again early if you want to come. Have laid in supply of Dramamine. P.S. Call Sheriff Z. D. Packa at Palm Beach. They found a skiff up there. Could be your fish lady's."

Alex turned that one over in his hand. A bit of good news for Chicago. Maybe now she would fling her arms around his neck and smother him with grateful kisses. Right.

He let his mind wander back to the dive. It was nice to be underwater, a feeling almost like flying. It was the closest he had felt to this enigmatic lady since he met her. She seemed so peaceful underwater. Well, for one thing she couldn't swear at him, but it was more than that; it was just a different way of being.

It was a shame the reef was so trashed there. There was so much garbage, shiploads of garbage. Shiploads of garbage! A new possible lead struck him, and if a light bulb could have appeared over his head, it would have been a hundred-watter. He grabbed the telephone and dialed Washington.

"Finneaus? Finneaus Freak of the Fabulous Furry Freak Brothers?"

"Hey, Alex, is that you? Where the hell are you? Mittens get down." Alex heard Finneaus swatting at something, then a solid thump as his twenty-pound cat plopped down from wherever she shouldn't have been. The sound made him homesick. It was six-thirty; Finneaus must have just gotten in from work.

"Still in Miami."

"So you find any of those *Miami Vice* babes, the ones in lycra?"

"Oh, buddy, there's flocks, but you know they're not my type."

"Hey, Cape Canaveral's down there—go find yourself a sexy rocket scientist and send me the vapid, materialistic well-built airheads."

"What would Jacquie have to say about that?" Alex said, laughing, referring fondly to Finneaus's gorgeous red-haired girl-friend.

"She'd say find her one, too. They come in both sexes, don't they? Hey, listen to this . . ."

Alex immediately held the receiver away from his ear. Whenever Finneaus said, "Listen to this," it was followed by an ear-splitting electric-guitar riff. Finneaus was not your typical Washington lawyer. True, he lived in Washington, wore a suit, and worked for the government, but he had managed to avoid the more pernicious aspects of the life.

Finneaus still lived in a group house (although a small one, with real furniture and no piles of dishes in the sink), played electric guitar in a band, and was thrilled recently when tie-dyes suddenly appeared on the street again. He worked for the EPA, stood six-six, and looked like Frank Zappa with Bambi's eyes. Alex had run into him, quite literally, one day on the Mt. Vernon bike trail when his front wheel caught a loose board on a bridge. They had shared a taxi to the hospital for stitches.

"Aiiiieeee! Yeah!" Finneaus finished with a few reverberating swipes. "So what's up?"

"I'm working on something down here and I need some expert advice in your area."

"And what area is that—among the many, that is."

"Garbage."

"Alex, my friend, I haven't seen you in eight months and you call me about garbage?"

"I need to know about ships dumping garbage off Miami."

"What about it?"

"Is it much of a problem?"

"I'm sure it's done. I don't know how big a problem it is. Garbage disposal is expensive, and if there's anyway to avoid it, scum'll do it. Remember that oil-storage tanker that collapsed a couple of years ago in Pennsylvania? Dumped some million gallons of oil in the Monongahela River? Well, as soon as the factories and chemical plants heard that, they opened the valves. Knew we couldn't trace their shit because of the oil, so they saved a few thousand bucks that month on chemical-waste disposal. Happens every time there's flood stages on the river, too. Anytime they can get away with it."

"So how easy would it be to get away with it here?"

"I'll have to check out the regs. I'm not up on dumping. I'm in toxic waste these days, but I would think the big ships are pretty well monitored."

"Good. I'm looking for a small ship. Can you find out if anyone's been cited or investigated for dumping garbage?"

"Sure, no problem. It'll take a couple of days. You got any names in particular?

"I wish I did. This whole thing's just a bunch of guesses." They talked for a few more minutes. Alex could hear Finneaus opening a can of cat food and rummaging around in the refrigerator as they talked. He wanted to know more about regular things, about Finneaus's semi-fiancée Jacquie, a teacher who made you long to be in second grade again. Alex looked up to see

Captain Torrance at his door. He had his tie loosened and brief-case in hand. He was leaving for the day but obviously wanted to talk to Alex first.

"Finn, I've got to go. I'll call you in a couple of days—right."

Torrance looked worn and gaunt but strangely animated. Per-haps it was just the evening sunlight streaming in the window that caught him at an odd angle. His eyes were a little too bright, in a way that made Alex uneasy. It was an excited, anxious, slightly mad sheen that an ordinary person, if he noticed it at all, would recognize from a blood-lust racquet ball player or a junior high school principal during the last week of term.

"They got Morales," he stated simply. "I'm sure you've heard by now. Two shots from a .38 revolver. Broad daylight. Just out-side the safe house."

Alex nodded and showed no response. His mind was already working. What did this mean? How did it fit in?

"There was no attempt to make it look accidental."

"So we have a leak?" Alex asked.

Torrance shrugged. "These guys, they seem to know every-thing." He paused and patted his pockets as if looking for keys. "I'm not sure how this will hurt your investigation, but I told Wonton we'll meet on it first thing tomorrow."

Alex nodded. The captain left, and Alex got up. He adjusted the blinds to cut the low glare and watched until Torrance came into view in the parking lot below. There were still too many people around the station, but perhaps later he could look around. He turned back to the papers on his desk and sifted through them for another twenty minutes, but distraction had set in. He stood and stretched, then decided to walk down to the lab and see if they had anything ready for him.

After they had found the corroded scuba tank that afternoon, Alex's hunch made a lot more sense. Cocaine could be smuggled inside the tanks, dropped off a passing ship, and later retrieved from shore. No one would think to inspect a day-charter boat out for a pleasure dive.

Finding the beat-up tank that afternoon was a good clue. Alex knew that if there was corrosion on the outside of the tank, there was probably some on the inside as well. He knew that if a scuba tank isn't at least partly full of compressed air, some air from the atmosphere inevitably leaks in. Compressed air is bone-dry, but regular air has enough moisture to start rust. If an empty tank is kept underwater without a regulator attached, a little water is bound to leak in, too. Traces of rust or saltwater on the bags would be good evidence that the cocaine had indeed been transported inside the scuba tanks. He had asked the lab to test the bags from the fish market bust.

He walked the long hallways and galloped down the stairs to the basement. The lab smelled and sounded like a high school chemistry class; there was a kind of acrid smell and a slight background hum. Two lab assistants looked up in surprise. They were the night crew and unused to company. Detectives didn't usually come down after their own reports. In fact, few people came even in the daytime. Information was generally blipped up and down to faceless screens or typed in triplicate on multicolored forms and filed in baskets for distribution by the appropriate peon.

"Hi, I'm Detective Sanders. I wonder if you have that analysis ready for me yet."

One scientist looked up at Alex through a glass forest of test tubes; the other's face was cast with a green hue from a spectrum chronographer. Clearly, they did not know how to respond.

"I—ah, needed to stretch my legs," Alex explained, sensing that he had breached some rule of etiquette but clueless as to which one. "I figured I would just run down here and pick it up."

"I don't know if you can do that, sir."

"It's not ready?"

The test tube scientist ignored him, picked up a capillary tube, and began dropping drops of one thing into another. The other man pushed his chair back, straightened his lab coat, and smoothed his hair back on both sides as if this were a visit by a minor royal figure or a tax auditor.

"Certainly it's ready. But the proper procedures require distribution of all forms to their appropriate offices. I can't just let you take it. Your office only gets the blue and white copies, yellow goes to records, pink to accounting, goldenrod—well, I'm not sure about goldenrod, but it goes somewhere."

"Well, what if I just take the blue and white and leave the rest of the rainbow right here?" Alex offered with a laugh, thinking it was a little joke.

The man thought about this. "I'm sorry, I'm afraid you just can't do that," he insisted, and Alex recognized the tyranny of the middle manager.

"Well, what if I just photocopied it and left all the colors here?" he asked with a cheerfulness strained through clenched teeth.

"No can do. Unauthorized reproduction."

Alex didn't know whether to laugh or stuff this guy in a petri dish.

"Okay. How about I just have the damn report tattooed across your ass and you can stand on your head while I read it?"

"There's no need to get aggressive, Detective Sanders. You hotshot gumshoes may think it's all your tough-guy gunslinging that gets the scum off the streets of our city, but you forget about the real work that goes on down here behind the glamour."

Christ, Alex thought, could he wedge just one more cliché into that sentence?

"I was just about to say that I'll be happy to let you read the report right here. Take notes if you like! And your own permanent copy will be delivered as per usual tomorrow morning."

The technician held out the multipage document as if it were the Magna Charta. Alex squelched his annoyance and took the report. He noted with satisfaction that they had found traces of rust on the cellophane bags. He left the lab in almost a good mood.

It wasn't until he got back to his desk that one other fact registered. He had only glanced at the composition figures on this latest report and they seemed normal: 45–50 percent pure cocaine, plus lidocaine, Enfamil, and other additives. What was wrong with that? Of course. Alex flipped through his files. He found a copy of the analysis from the day of the bust. That day, the coke was 90 percent pure.

He threw the file onto the desk, swept the paperwork into a sloppy pile, and slumped into his seat. "Shit." He was getting so involved in this minor smuggling scheme that he was forgetting his real business here. Alex hurled his pen across the room, where it stabbed arrowlike through one fat leaf of the abused rubber plant. He felt immediately sorry and removed the pen, rubbing the wounded leaf. How many officers could have had access to the seized drugs? Were they part of the core group or just new opportunists? He knew of several cops who had stolen drugs before. He would have to run them down, go back to the lab—he groaned at the thought—and see if he could get prints off the bag.

Alex suddenly didn't want to think about it anymore. He had been told this was a relatively straightforward case—routine corruption, like shaking a rug. The people at the Bureau had almost all the material evidence they needed, they just wanted to boost their case with an insider who could testify and tie up the loose ends. So they had said.

He thought about doing a quick search of Torrance's office, but it was still early. Besides that, he was just plain tired of it. He wanted to feel the peace of being underwater again. Down there it was so quiet. No one could touch you. What he really wanted was to fly again, not in the fast planes and helicopters he had known the last ten years, but in the planes of long-ago flying.

He wanted to come in low over the swirls and rows of just-plowed fields, then climb up above the clouds into the sun. He wanted to fly slow loops, maybe head over to the lake and skim the water. He closed his eyes and remembered the incredible thrill he felt the first time he soloed in the crop duster. Compared to the planes he had flown since then, it was like driving a milk truck, but there was a plane you could really feel under your hands.

He pushed away from the desk. It was time for speed, time to be a machine. A few minutes later he swung onto his bicycle and coasted out into the night air. Well, even if he had to be miserable, he could at least make one person happy. Chicago would get her boat back. Who knows, it might mean the end of the cold war.

Chapter 15

Chicago was eating dinner on deck, alternately stabbing black olives out of the can with an awl and taking bites of a banana. She did this by touch, since she was engrossed in a book. A filament lantern sputtered softly close by. Alex coasted up, came to a stop, and leaned on his handlebars.

"Shucks, I was going to invite you to dinner, but I see I can't hope to match that repast."

"You again."

"No, no, it goes, 'Why, Alex, I missed you. Come on in. You're welcome to join me.' "

"Why, Alex, I missed you. You're welcome to join me," she responded tartly, but with a suggestion of warmth.

"Do I need my own tool?" Alex leaned his bicycle against a piling and pulled off his shoes so as not to scuff her deck.

"No, I'll just drop them in the bilge and you can bob for them."

"Is that really dinner?"

"What are you, taking a survey?"

"Yeah, I'm Captain Nutrition policing the four major food groups. Give me an olive?"

She handed him the can.

"Not much for cooking, are you?"

"It's the one job I refused to learn on ship. Too easy to get stuck doing it. Anyway, food's food."

"Well, the way I see it, this food ain't food. Anyplace we can get a sandwich or something?"

"There's a take-out place up the road a little way. If you let me finish this chapter."

"Fine, I can wait, I just hope I don't forget to tell you about a certain beat-up crummy old motorboat that drifted into Palm Beach a few days ago . . ."

"You're kidding! Is it true?" Chicago dropped the book, fairly leapt from the cockpit, and grabbed his arms. "My boat! Is it mine for sure?"

"I doubt there are many other beat-up old skiffs floating around Palm Beach."

"When can we get it?"

"Let's get my sandwich, and I'll tell you all about it."

She pulled on her sneakers and jumped up onto the dock.

"Some yachties found it a couple of days ago," Alex explained as they walked. "The drifting anchor rope had snagged on someone's dinghy in the harbor—probably thought it would try to mate and ruin the pedigree."

"Must've got caught in the Gulf Stream."

"Thank Wonton, really. He's got friends all up and down the coast. I'm sure that helped."

The world was suddenly a good place as far as Chicago was concerned. Without the boat, her enterprises had been severely limited.

The neon sign for KING KONG'S BURGER JUNGLE flashed through the palm trees. It was bright inside, with fluorescent lighting and white tile. Two young punkish couples slouched in the only booth. The table between them looked like a war zone of ketchup-stained wrappers and sacrificed french fries. The man behind the counter looked bored and tubercular.

"Relax, I've eaten here a lot," Chicago whispered.

"Somehow that doesn't exactly reassure me."

They bought sandwiches and started back to the *Tassia Far,* the warm scent of meatball subs drifting out of the bag. The air was cool and the stars were bright in the moonless sky. The only sound was the gentle lapping of water and the slow creak of moored boats. Halfway down the dock, however, the quiet was suddenly broken by a slight but ominous clink and the quick scuff of boots. Two men leapt from the shadows.

Alex felt their presence before he saw it—a solid, aggressive mass in motion. He ducked instinctively as a chain whistled inches from his head. With a fast swooping kick he landed a solid blow to the unseen attacker. A whumphing groan announced good contact. It sounded like bread dough being punched, but a huge, solid lump of bread dough, pumpernickel or rye. Alex lunged toward the sound with a graceful but deadly motion, hurling his head down and delivering another kick. The movement looked as much a dance as a martial art, something that Bruce Lee might choreograph for Baryshnikov. The flesh he hit was fairly soft, but there was a lot of it there. Alex could tell the guy was out of shape but not totally washed up in the thug business.

A string of curses in one familiar and one unknown but nasty-sounding voice told Alex that Chicago was in trouble, too. A second man had grabbed her from behind. The struggling pair was back-lit by the lamp on the end of the pier, and it was hard to see, but the man's silhouette was roughly the size of King Kong of Jungle Burger fame.

What is this attack from land of the giants? Alex thought. The man had Chicago in a bear hug, and her arms were pinned to her sides. He had lifted her feet clear off the ground, but she was kicking violently at his shins.

She struggled to break his grip and finally wriggled one arm up, secured one of his fingers, and yanked it violently. She felt with satisfaction the bone snap out of its joint. At the same time she jerked her head back as hard as she could, slamming her resolute skull against the more fragile chin of her attacker. The man yelped in pain and shards of teeth spilled into her hair, like peanuts from a bag.

The man staggered backward, and Chicago fell dazed against a dock pylon. She saw Alex, with the same dancelike form, throw himself into a sort of handless cartwheel toward the man, kicking him three times in a blurred scissor kick, finishing with a final lock on his ankles that brought him crashing to the dock.

Alex rolled immediately up again, balanced on the balls of his feet, ready for the first assailant to lunge, looking for any others, and listening for the click of a gun. He felt his fingertips tingling and was aware of the sharp smell of his own sweat. This was different from cycling sweat, different from basketball in the hot sun sweat. This sweat was acrid and thin; it was like tannin in a swamp, like the blood in a hornet. This sweat stretched his skin and made it sensitive, like the hairs on a carnivorous plant.

He blocked the next blow easily, although the tail of the chain whipped around his head and opened a gash below his right ear. He caught the arm and pulled. It was the size of a Sunday roast. With a twisting jerk, Alex flipped the man to the boards, dropping his own body into a somersault to avoid the swinging chain.

Chicago, meanwhile, had snatched a boat hook off the deck of a yacht and was raining blows on whomever was nearest. Both men were up again, and Alex met their renewed attack with a flurry of round-off kicks, lightning-fast but oddly graceful.

Lights were coming on in a few of the boats, and Alfred, the night patrolman, was running toward them, waving his nightstick and shouting. Suddenly, one of the attackers managed to grab the pole from Chicago and yanked it out of her hands. Alex saw the boat hook swinging toward Chicago and dived toward her, flinging his body between her and the weapon.

It's aluminum, asshole! flashed through his mind as he imagined the mockery Chicago could heap on him for the dramatic save when none was needed. They fell to the dock together, Alex's body shielding hers, but the aluminum pole only left a taunting sting as it smacked across his shoulders. It was the kicks that really hurt, a series of fast, hard, heavy-booted kicks to his kidneys. The stomp on the head didn't help much, either. Through the blinding pain he felt a trickle of grit running into his ear. The two assailants took off, running.

Alex gasped, trying to catch his breath. He pressed his face against the weathered boards of the dock. They were still warm from the day and smelled of salt and creosote. Chicago rolled out from under his arm and almost pounced on him with concern, a little rough for concern, but genuine.

"Alex, are you dead?" she gasped, turning him over. The movement sent stabs of pain through his body.

"Ow! No," he whispered hoarsely. "Just . . . a minute. I'm fine." The boards vibrated wildly as Alfred came running up, his flashlight bobbing. Great, Alex thought, I need a stretcher and I get a xylophone.

"Are you all right, Miss Chicago?"

She rubbed the back of her head and squinted irately into the flashlight beam.

"Ooops, I'm sorry." Alfred swung the beam out of her face. "If you're all right, I'll go call the police," he offered.

"That's okay." Alex groaned. "Don't bother."

"Okay. Who the hell are you?" she demanded fiercely, once they got below deck to the security of the *Tassia Far.*

"Temporary amnesia isn't unusual after a blow to the head," Alex replied dourly as he wrung out a towel and held it to the cut behind his ear. "Got any ice?"

She stood resolutely in the middle of the cabin, arms folded.

Her voice shook a little, but she had that look again, the look that could quell mutinies and freeze a vulture's blood. Her clothes were dirty, one sleeve was ripped, and her hair was speckled with bits of teeth.

"I mean it, Alex. If that's really your name."

"What are you talking about?"

"*Capoeira*. Don't tell me they teach obscure Brazilian martial arts at the Pierce County YMCA."

Alex shut off the faucet and leaned against the galley door. The sudden tension between them was a solid force, like magnetic repulsion.

"*Capoeira?*" He feigned puzzlement. It was pretty obscure, all right. He was shocked that she had recognized it. *Capoeira* was developed in the mid 1800s by Brazilian slaves. It was based on movements, mostly kicks, that could be performed with one's hands tied. Later, slaves who had escaped to the mountains refined it, incorporating dance and acrobatics with karatelike kicks to develop this beautiful and deadly art.

"I saw it at a folk festival once." He shrugged.

"Bullshit! And today wasn't the first time you went scuba diving, either!"

Alex felt the back of his neck start to prickle, but he forced his voice to keep its casual tone.

"How else was I going to get a date with you?"

"Can it, you shit!" Chicago hurled the shrunken head at him, then reached quickly behind the chart table and pulled out a knife.

"You better give me some straight answers. We just got jumped and you've got more lies dangling off you than a political campaign."

Alex considered for a second that she might be able to throw the knife with the same accuracy she had demonstrated with stones and shrunken heads, but he decided to call her bluff. He walked slowly into the cabin, palms up, breaking the force field. He watched her hand for the slightest reflex. The knife had a six-inch blade and a carved handle. She held it as if she knew how to use it. He stopped a few feet away.

"You should have learned, with the boat hook, never to introduce a weapon unless you're sure you can hold on to it."

"I'm shaking like Snow White in the forest," she snapped sarcastically. But she *was* shaking, Alex noticed, and she backed away a step. Her eyes were sharp. Icy blue, like a huskie's. Her whole body was tense. She was scared.

He didn't need that; didn't like it, either. He knew how to scare people well enough. "Sit down," he said, and dropped carelessly onto the huge overstuffed sofa, wincing with the pain in his ribs. "I'm one of the good guys."

"So give me some damn good answers."

"I guess you're not the sort who can take 'trust me, baby' for an answer? I didn't think so." He stretched his long legs out as if he were slouching in for a football game. "So sit down, will you. Haven't we had enough dramatics for one night?"

Chicago slowly eased into a deck chair opposite him, laying the knife down in her lap.

"I learned *capoeira* in Peru, from an old Brazilian guerilla buddy. I learned to dive in the navy. I can't tell you exactly what I'm doing here, but I am on the side of truth, justice, and the American way. I have no idea who those goons were. I haven't, to my knowledge, made those sorts of enemies yet."

"What were you doing in Peru?"

"Infiltrating the Shining Path." Alex rather enjoyed the bluntness of that bombshell, but if she was at all affected (or impressed), she didn't show it.

"And Guatemala?" Now it was Alex's turn to look at her suspiciously.

"The shirt you said was a gift from a friend was tailored to fit you."

"So he got the fabric and I had it made here."

"Wrong. It was sewn on a manual treadle machine. I could tell by the stitching."

Alex smiled and nodded, respecting her sharpness. "Very good, Nancy Drew. Guatemala was . . . just along the way."

"To where?"

"You're getting pretty nosey."

"Are you CIA?"

Alex paused a beat, decided he could answer the question honestly in its strictest sense: are you (now) CIA?

"No," he replied evenly.

"Why should I believe you?"

"Why does it matter?"

"I don't trust government goons and I don't trust glorious assholes. Double reason."

The banter was curiously exciting, something like delightful. She was sharp and she was ripping him apart. It felt great.

"I have in the past worked for organizations with initials," he admitted.

"And I'll bet it wasn't the ACLU."

Alex laughed.

"So you're not really a cop?"

Alex considered that one for a few seconds. "I really am a cop. For the time being."

"So why did you lie about the diving?" she persisted.

"What gave me away?"

"Your buoyancy was too good, too automatic. You felt for hair around the skirt of your mask the first time you were adjusting it; novices don't think of that. And you took your regulator out to rinse your mouth once. No one does that on their first dive.

People on their first dive hold on so tight they bite through the mouthpiece," she finished with a hint of smugness.

"Damn." Alex sighed in genuine admiration.

"So why did you try to fake it?"

"It didn't really fit Alex Sanders's mild-mannered Midwestern profile."

"Is any of that real?"

"A good cover never makes up more than necessary; too easy to slip up. Yes, I am from the geographical center of North America and I did play tuba in the high school band. I do have four sisters, a regular, if enormous, family and a slightly irregular grandmother."

Chicago thought about this for a minute, and he couldn't tell if she was believing him or not.

"So how did you wind up doing . . . whatever," she pressed him. Alex leaned his head back and looked around the snug salon. He had to think about that one. It was something he was trying to forget. Something to be done with. But he owed her some explanation. When he spoke, his voice was terse.

"I enlisted in the navy when I was seventeen. The draft was slowing down, but I had a low number. Mostly, I just wanted some adventure. I wanted to get out of North Dakota. I had never seen an ocean, so I picked the Navy, but I was already a flyer. I got my pilot's license pretty young. My uncle flew crop dusters. So anyway, they kept me flying. The Vietnam War was winding down by the time I got there. I never really saw combat. I wound up crop-dusting the jungles for a few months. Then toward the end, there was a lot of . . . tidying up that needed doing."

Alex paused. Chicago was watching him intently, skeptically. There was too much he couldn't explain.

"I was a good pilot, good for certain things, that is. I was given small planes, and I flew around and picked up people here and there, intelligence people," he explained. "I was smart. I was

patriotic. After the war I was offered other . . . opportunities."
He paused as if searching for the words, as if he were wondering
himself just how in hell it had all happened.

"Spy stuff?" she probed.

"Sometimes." Alex sighed. He was feeling uncomfortable with
the whole subject. First of all, he hadn't had to tell anyone about
his past for a long time, second, the "spy business" had lost all
glamour as aspects of its unsavory past had been revealed over the
years. Even a GS 12 file clerk for the CIA got heat for moral
compromise these days.

"I was a free agent. I worked on a lot of different projects."

"Projects," she repeated flatly. Alex felt a slight relief. He
didn't really hear that tone, that self-righteous accusing How
could you be part of something like that? tone that crept into
most speeches about clandestine government groups. She just
sounded surprised.

"Stuff like Ollie North and those guys, that Iran contra stuff?"
she asked, still not sure how much of his story she believed, or
wanted to.

"That wasn't really my turf," Alex answered with a bitter
smile. "But let's just say nothing in that whole affair surprised me
much."

Chicago leaned back in the deck chair, looked around the
cabin, digesting all this. Absently, she spun the knife on the little
table. Alex felt strung out, in need of air. There was a rumbling
inside him, like a plane about to take off, and he wanted to push
it down.

"I got out of that finally," he continued, meeting her gaze,
wanting desperately, he realized, for her not to hate him now,
"about a year ago. Things were getting a little crazy. I spent two
years undercover in Central America—flying." Alex caught himself. He felt a huge weight pressing at the back of his brain and
was afraid to go any farther. It was put away, it was contained and

slowly dissolving away in its secret compartment; he couldn't let it out now.

"Everything there was pretty crazy." He squeezed his eyes shut and rubbed his aching head. There was a warm stickiness on the side of his neck and he realized the cut had started bleeding again.

"Are you really all right?" Chicago asked. (By God, was there a note of compassion in her voice?)

"Yeah," he said, eyes opening quickly, almost startled. He sat up a little and shook his head to clear the last of the dirt out of his ear.

"Here, let me see." She crossed the cabin with only a trace of hesitancy and knelt on the sofa beside him. They sat frozen for what seemed a long time, then she gently turned his head a little toward the light and wiped the blood from the gash. Alex reached up and put his hand on top of hers, feeling the wet cloth through her fingers. He turned back so he could see her face.

A stalemated silence hung between them, the only sound a soft rustle behind the books as Lassie slithered from *The Complete Works of William Shakespere* to *Jaws*. Chicago's body gave off a cushion of heat. Alex could see a sheen of sweat glistening in the hollow of her neck and on her chest where her blouse was torn. She smelled like wood, salt, boots, and danger. She was trembling just a little; he could feel it in her hand.

Alex reached up and plucked a bit of broken tooth from her hair. He smiled and held it out on his palm. Chicago looked at the fragment and her eyes filled with tears. No sobbing, no hysterics; there were just these silent, still tears and a deep trembling, as if she had been plucked from below ice.

Suddenly, he felt how awfully long and slammed together the day had been. Alex pulled her to him and buried his face in the mane of hair, where it was hot and damp from her neck. He could feel her fingers clutching the nape of his neck, pulling steadily on his hair as she pressed against him. They were like stones in the surf, scraped and buffed and skins humming. Cradled in the antique couch, their bodies caressed by the silky brocade, they made love, desperately and fast.

Chapter 16

The sun streamed in through the hatch, and Alex squinted, turned away, then woke with a start and bolted upright, startled to find himself in a strange place.

"You always wake up like that?" Chicago teased from the doorway. She was freshly out of the shower, wearing a sarong and toweling her hair dry.

Alex slumped back onto the pillows. His heart was racing. Yes, he often woke up that way, even in his own bed. His throat was dry and his head felt like a rodeo. He reached toward the site of the worst throbbing and felt a bulky dressing where Chicago had bandaged the wound.

He shut his eyes and took a few deep breaths, opened his eyes again, and looked around. The bow cabin was cozy and remarkably feminine, with flowered sheets and an abundance of Chicago's woven pillows in pastel shades. An old-fashioned chenille bedcover was draped over him. The V-shaped bunk filled the whole space so it was a cozy little nook, just right for two.

Chicago came in and sat on the edge of the bed. Alex closed his eyes again and let the scent of her fill the air—wet hair and Pears soap and just plain warm skin smells. He reached for her, and she came willingly into his arms, lay half curled beside him with her head on his chest. A heavy lock of wet hair fell across his face and he had an urge to chew on it.

"How do you feel?" she asked softly.

"I don't know. How do I feel?" Alex responded, pulling her on top of him. She laughed, a low whiskey laugh, a very sexy laugh. She kissed him, soft but deep, like eating a handful of hibiscus flowers. He fought the urge to open his eyes and lost himself in the kissing, biting her lip when she tried to stop. He reached up and touched her bare shoulders, then slid his hands down the smooth skin of her arms all the way to her fingertips. She made a little sound, a spiderweb sound, and leaned back.

Alex began to feel her body through the light cloth, his touch lingering at each curve, slipping up under her breasts, everything delicious and slow. Chicago leaned her head back, letting the warm sun fall on her chest. Alex opened his eyes. She looked like a cougar, drunk in the feeling. He tugged at the sarong and it fell open, the multicolored cloth spreading out around her like some tropical bird.

Their eyes met and she smiled. The sheltered skin of her breasts was whiter than he had thought it would be; it was a pale golden shade, like cream from a Jersey cow.

"Hey—" she said softly. "So . . . can I at least know your name?"

"Alexander."

"Alexander . . . that's all I can know?"

He shook his head. "That's all there is."

"No last name?"

"I lost it. Put it down one day and must've forgotton where."

He half sat up and pulled her close. She pressed her body into his, kissing him deeply. She wondered if he could feel her heart pounding. She had thought about making love to him and the thought had unnerved her. Now she didn't think about it. She just lost herself in the sun warmth and the feel of his skin. She bent toward him, took his chin in her mouth. This made him laugh, and she could feel his penis, already hard, leap up a little against her. She tightened her legs around him. She kissed her way along his neck and nipped his ear with her lips. Alex pressed his hips up against her and felt her shudder. He ran his hands down her back. It was a wonderful back, broad and muscular. A little more overall padding would not have hurt her figure, he thought as he pressed the soft flesh, but what was here was nicely arranged.

Chicago slowly rolled up again and looked at him. Alex felt a twinge of wariness. He couldn't read her. Her body, her movement, was sensual and eager, but now something in her eyes hesitated. Some sadness or fear haunted her. He drew his hands back and took hold of hers. No good if it felt wrong. But she smiled, a dreamy welcoming smile.

"Alexander Good-enov" she teased. She leaned back a little and lifted her arms, curling her fingers around the overhead storm rail. Slowly, she drew herself up just enough for Alex to pull away the thin spread that still separated half their bodies.

"So let's talk about last night," Alex suggested as he watched Chicago make coffee.

"It was good for me. Was it good for you?" she responded flippantly.

"That's not what I meant. Have there been an unusual number of muggings in this neighborhood lately?"

"Alex." Chicago brought him a mug of coffee and set a loaf of bread and jam on the table. There was a hint of guilt in her expression. "I think . . . maybe I know why those men jumped us." She took a deep breath and looked at the table, rolling a stray breadcrumb under one finger. "I was just getting around to telling you."

"So tell me," Alex responded, catching her finger between his. She pulled it away again.

"After we found the corroded tank yesterday afternoon, I—I talked to George Tessely. He came to pick up his tanks. He looked surprised to see that one; I think it got in there by mistake. Anyway, I told him I knew what he was doing . . ."

Alex's heart jumped a little. "And—" he prompted.

". . . And I told him I was interested in a piece of the action. I told him I knew what he was doing and I wanted him to cut me in or I would go to the police."

"That was stupid," Alex replied bluntly after a second's pause. "And we *don't* know what he's doing!"

"The hell we don't. He damn well isn't crocheting afghans for the church bazaar!"

"Well, he also damn well isn't about to just let you join his club! What—why did you do that?" Alex was angry and gave her no time to reply. "What the hell were you trying to do?"

"Well, shit on you, Sherlock!" She swung away angrily. "What was I supposed to do, wait around for the fucking cops to do something when you wouldn't even believe anything was wrong? I had to do something, and it seemed like a good plan."

"Seemed like?" he shouted. "Seemed like is for It seemed like a nice day! or That horse seemed like a winner. It's not for *plans.* You don't just go with a plan that *seems* good!"

Alex got up and paced the small cabin. He stopped and stood with his back to her, leaning against the companionway ladder, staring up into the morning that had started out so well. "So what exactly did you plan on doing?"

Chicago replied coolly, "I'll go along on the dive with them when they pick up the cocaine, then you can arrest them and I'll testify."

"Right."

"Goddamnit, Alex, what the hell was I supposed to do?"

"Nothing! How about just pure nothing? Why the hell do you need to do anything at all?"

"Because someone has to, and you weren't."

"Goddamnit yourself, it's not that simple! You're talking about joining a drug dealer, not the Camp Fire girls!"

"Well, what the hell plan did you have?"

"My plan," he said tensely, "was to find out who's bringing the stuff in, who's supplying it, who's distributing it here, catch them all, and stay alive in the process. Your little adventures in home crime solving could blow all that."

Alex slammed his fist against the wall. Maybe it was something about him that just attracted complications. "Shit. Well, so what now? What did he say when you told him?"

"Mostly nothing—told me I was nuts and shit like that."

"Well, he obviously isn't eager to have you sign up." He rubbed the back of his neck, where the throbbing had suddenly begun anew. "That was a pretty clear warning we got."

Chicago stood up but didn't speak.

"Does anyone around here know I'm a cop besides you and Umbi?"

She shook her head.

"Don't publicize it. It can't help your popularity with Tessely. And stay here today."

Chicago nodded, took the cups to the sink, and began to wipe the table with violent sweeps of a rag.

"I have to go. I'm late."

Chicago said nothing.

"Stay here." Alex climbed up the companionway ladder without a backward glance and unlocked his bicycle from the dock. He looked over the *Tassia Far* and thought briefly about sabotaging it in some way to keep her stuck there for a week or so, until things cooled off. Maybe super-glue all over the deck. Naw, she was the type who would cut her own foot off.

He wheeled his bicycle along the dock. He had to admit that infiltrating Tessely's operation was what he had had in mind. But besides the fact that she was a goddamn hothead, Alex now had personal reasons for keeping Chicago out of it.

Chapter 17

Umbi was running down the dock as Alex left.

"Hey, mon, what happen? Old Al say Chicago beat up last night!"

"She's okay. She's on her boat."

"She ain't hurt?"

"She's too hardheaded."

"Mon, you beat up yourself! You look like you head been through some rocks."

"Yeah." Alex didn't feel like going into it. "Got any plans today?"

"I'll see for myself that Chicago's okay, then . . ." He shrugged. "I don't know."

"Good. I've got a job for you." Alex pulled out a couple of twenties. "You're her bodyguard. Don't let her out of your sight."

Umbi looked surprised, then hurt. "Hey, Chicago my friend. That ain't a job for money, mon. What's going on? She in trouble?"

"Knee-deep, and she's in head first. Just stick with her. Don't tell her I asked you to."

"You don't need to ask me. I be doing it anyway. I figure she don't get jumped on by no friends and neighbors."

"Well, here, take this anyway—for lunch. The galley's bare."

He pressed one bill into Umbi's hand and pushed past him out the gate before the boy could object. When he stepped on the pedal and started to swing his leg over the seat, a stab of pain shot through his side. Funny, Alex thought as he mounted more gingerly, it hadn't hurt that much this morning.

It was a strange day. The sun didn't last. Clouds blew in off the sea and settled with a misty silence over Miami. The sky was heavy and low. On the beach, the sandpipers quit their individual zigzagging and gathered in restless bunches, screeching into the air, then settling down nervously some distance away. Retirees sitting in rows on hotel porches buttoned their cardigans and talked about the chill, mentioning various friends and relatives who had died after taking a chill on a day like this. Around eleven o'clock, the wind picked up, and they left the porches in twos and threes to play canasta or watch TV before lunch.

The grumpy children of families on vacation, who would rather have stayed in Disney World and not even come here in the first place, were bored and whiny. The video-game machines ate a lot of quarters.

The prostitutes coming off a long night's work lingered through the gray morning in the coffee shops, filling ashtrays and getting jittery from too much caffeine. The VFW #42 from Milwaukee got off its airplane at Miami International and upon stepping outside said things like, "I told you so," and "I hope the hotel has cable."

Chicago sat at her loom, sliding the shuttle back and forth, rhythmically pressing the treadle with one foot, concentrating on the pattern and the feel of cloth. The wooden clack of the frame was her mantra. The loom, grand and imposing as a cathedral, occupied most of the aft cabin on the *Tassia Far.* The rest of the space held baskets full of wool and silk, bright fat spools of cotton thread, jars of beads, feathers, and animal claws, boxes of scraps, bits of something waiting to become something else through her weaving. Lassie rested contently on top of a pile of yarn. The snake had shed recently and its body was sleek and bright; iridescent shades of purple and green were noticeable in the black markings.

Umbi napped outside on the sofa, a study manual for the GED open on his chest, rising and falling slightly with each unscholarly breath.

This was Chicago's sanctuary, and right now she needed it badly. She could be lost here, lost in the rhythm and texture, lost in the pictures she wove in the tapestries. She could leave all the rough edges of life outside and find color and softness here. She could create beauty and a sort of perfection.

But now even her weaving was rough. She pulled too hard and a thread snapped. She dropped the shuttle and tangled it trying to pick up the pattern again. Finally, she just gave up. Her joy had vanished as thoroughly as the sun this morning. She left her bench and rolled her shoulders to ease the tightness, leaned against the loom, and looked out the narrow porthole. Eye-level with the dock—tide was out. She glanced at the bottom cabinets, then slowly eased down and sat on the cabin floor. With some hesitancy, she pushed aside two baskets of yarn, opened a drawer, and carefully pulled out a small bundle, a folded red sweater.

Chicago leaned against a basket of scraps in a comforting nook, surrounded by the colorful yarn, and stroked the sweater. She held it to her nose and sniffed it. By now it smelled only of wool, no longer of Stephen; but then Stephen had smelled kind of woolly himself, so the scent was the same.

She sat there for a long time thinking about Alex, and about Stephen. How should she feel now? Finally, she unwrapped the bundle. Inside, carefully cushioned by the sweater, were two photographs in an old hinged silver frame. In one, Stephen sat dripping wet and grinning broadly, astride *Banto,* the mini-sub from which he had just emerged. He was excited. They had just been five hundred feet down in a trench off Bermuda and had for the first time seen and filmed six-gill sharks. In the picture you could see him with one foot on the deck, one still in the sub, just climbing out. His hair was sun-bleached and wet.

In the other photo, he and Chicago were posed against the rail of a ship; his hair was dry and combed. They both wore brightly colored Bolivian Indian clothes embroidered all over with fish and ancient symbols. She held a single bird-of-paradise flower like a regal scepter. It was their wedding picture.

It was just over two years now since his death. Alex was her first . . . what was he, anyway? Chicago wasn't sure. Since Stephen's death, she had had two brief affairs—a short and ultimately sad "comfort" affair with an old friend and, just recently, a one-night stand with an eighteen-year old scuba student. She smiled at the memory of that. He was young and gorgeous, at the peak of bronzed athletic perfection, yet unassuming and sweet. He had been so excited about getting certified; he wanted to know every fish. He had made her laugh.

A good dive often made Chicago horny, and they had had a wonderful dive that day. He had helped her bring the tanks back and dropped one on her foot in the fill shack. It didn't hurt all that much, but he had dropped to his knees, put her foot in his lap, and kissed it, and well—there he was, fun, innocent, sexy. Probably a virgin, she thought later, and chuckled at the memories he would have—making love on a cushion of wet suits, with the compressor rattling away in the background. A few seconds after he came—with all the guts and glory of new manhood—a burst valve exploded on one of the tanks and scared him to death.

"But now," she said to the picture, touching the edge of Stephen's hair, "I don't know about this." Now there was more than just the need to be touched or the raw lust of sexual desire. For so long she had felt just the stupor of loss, a thick depression that left her aching and useless or drove her to wildness. Once, a few weeks after his death, she had gone out alone in her boat, out to where she knew it was deep, put on her scuba gear, and started swimming down, intending never to return. At three hundred feet, regular compressed air becomes toxic. It was this depth she had sought.

At a hundred fifty feet, nitrogen narcosis set in, that giddy, drunken feeling that nitrogen can cause at deeper depths. The water was so clear that day, she began to feel a sweet contentment, a very real sense of peace. But Chicago had told herself it was just the narcosis, and she determined to go on with it.

She swam deeper. She began to hear music in her bubbles, like brass chimes streaming out into the water, as she swam on down, looking for the deep blue of oblivion. The chimes grew louder and seemed to be filling the whole sea, calling her out, daring her, as Stephen had dared her, to live. At 190 she stopped, hovered in the crystal-blue emptiness of open sea, and felt some new, overpowering joy. It was her love for the sea, her mother ocean, Stephen's presence in this rare, perfect place that made her turn around. It wasn't right to make the ocean swallow her pain.

The healing had started that day, but not until this morning had she moved beyond simple healing to flourishing. Now, she thought sourly, I've probably fucked that up, too.

Chapter 18

"Whoa! What'ja do? Ride into a bus?" Wonton greeted Alex at the station.

"Something like that."

"Maybe you better switch to roller skates."

"We need to talk."

"Okay, talk."

Alex quickly sketched out the latest developments for his partner—the corroded scuba tank, his suspicions about the amount of garbage in the area, the lab-test results (leaving out the part about the recently diluted cocaine), and Chicago's involvement.

Wonton thought it all over, asked a few questions, scribbled some notes.

"So what's the problem? You don't like her plan?" He wasn't trying to be cavalier, but it sounded that way to Alex. "She's in a perfect position to do it. She's smart enough, and we already know she's tough enough. More importantly, we can't think of anything better."

"There's a million problems. She's not a cop. She's too goddamn hotheaded, and we can't give her any backup."

"C'mon, it's a little bust on a couple of little guys. It's not like we're dealing with the Medellín cartel. They're practically friends of hers."

Alex glared at him.

"Anyway, we can have some backup. We can be fishing nearby or something."

"Too suspicious. They know that no one fishes around Osprey."

"So we'll anchor farther out. What if we get a speedboat—" Wonton's eyes lit up as he started to devise a plan. "We could hide it behind an anchored trawler. The trawler would look like it was broken down or something. We could be a mile away and still get there in a couple of minutes if we have to. We can have plenty of backup." He leaned forward excitedly. "Yeah, we can *get* these guys!"

There was a knock on the door. Mrs. James Beaufort opened it and stepped inside.

"I'm sorry to interrupt, but, Detective Baxter sir, your wife called and said it was important to talk to you. No emergency, she said"—the way Mrs. James Beaufort said *emergency* let you know that in her long life she was familiar with the fact of it—"but she did ask you to come as soon as possible. She's at St. Jude's and said you knew where to call."

In an instant Wonton's whole person changed. He seemed to shrink and weaken. The joviality of a moment ago had vanished. He looked immensely sad but not really surprised.

"Thanks." He nodded to Mrs. James Beaufort as he rose from the chair. "Alex, I've got to go. We'll get back on this later. Uh, think about what I said. Check with Dalton in impoundment. I think there's a cigarette boat from a seizure in Ft. Lauderdale we could use . . ." he finished on his way out the door.

"I hope everything's all right." Mrs. James Beaufort patted his arm as he left.

Alex stared after him, totally puzzled, too surprised to have said anything. "Is Ellen okay? She's not hurt or anything?"

"Oh no, it's his son," Mrs. James Beaufort replied sadly. "And I think everything was going well for a while."

"Dusty?" Alex started. He had met Wonton's three-year-old and knew him as a sturdy child who regularly crashed into things and emerged laughing.

"Oh no, his older boy, Joseph."

Alex felt a pounding in his temples. Wonton had never mentioned another child. True, Alex had only known him for six months, but he had had no idea. Once he had been to Wonton's for a barbecue, and a couple of times he was in the house coming or going somewhere, but the only pictures he recalled were some standard department-store-studio shots of Dusty.

"Is St. Jude's a children's hospital?" Alex asked, trying to get a little information without exposing his ignorance of the matter. He felt embarrassed and deficient not to have known this.

"I'm sorry, sir. I thought you knew. But then Detective Baxter doesn't talk about him anymore. I'm not sure how much I should say. Poor child was born with . . . special problems. They kept him home for a couple of years—let's see, he must be around nine now—but then I think it was just too hard on Mrs. Baxter." Mrs. James Beaufort stopped then and blushed a little. "I don't feel it's my place—"

"No, of course not. Thank you, Mrs. James Beaufort." Alex rose politely. "I'm sure things will work out okay," he added lamely as he held the door for her. Sure? He wasn't sure of anything anymore. In fifteen minutes and a few phone calls, Alex had all the information he needed on St. Jude's but only a little more insight into Wonton.

St. Jude's was a well-respected private hospital, one of the only facilities in the state that cared for severely retarded and autistic children. It had a waiting list of over three hundred, with an average wait of four years. Residential treatment and care cost almost $100,000 a year. There was no mention of it in the police-department dossier on Frank Baxter.

Damn! Alex paced the room, then sat on the edge of his desk with his feet on the windowsill. A few days ago it had seemed that the whole thing might be wrapped up soon. Why had he let it get this tangled? He didn't know where to go with it now. He felt divided between the corruption investigation and this drug bust. Why was Chicago so eager to get messed up with these guys, anyway? And why was he so eager? It was, as Wonton had said, a little bust on a couple of little guys. If he could track down the ship and keep Chicago's plan delayed for a few weeks, maybe they could get Tessely some other way.

Meanwhile, he could only wait and keep busy. Tonight he would go over the new files, pull together the tightest cases for Washington, and maybe put together some of the missing pieces on Torrance. And Wonton, he remembered sourly. Now Wonton, too. Alex felt the dull ache of depression surround his skull and start to squeeze. So he can't be your friend—so big deal, do the job, he told himself.

According to various Agency psychologists who had inter-viewed and examined him throughout his career, Alex had any number and assortment of personality disorders. Depending on the craziness of his last undercover assignment, the shrink's mood at the time, and probably solar flares, they had declared him everything from a passive-aggressive avoidant with borderline per-sonality disorder to compulsive schizotypal to downright nuts.

He had always been something of a loner but not in any way antisocial. He had strong family ties and a few close friends, but he had a stronger sense that he was somehow still removed. His friends would have been surprised to know that Alex had always felt himself just on the fringe of everything, an observer. He had never been excluded; if anything, he was usually the leader in a group, though in such an unconscious way that others would not even notice it. He could fit easily in any group. It was in fact his uncanny ability to do this that had made him so successful in his career. He could be—had been, in fact—rich man, poor man, beggerman, thief, and he knew Indian chief wouldn't be much of a problem either. Yet despite all this, Alex had always felt some vast aloneness.

It was the nature of the work, he told himself. Close, intense relationships in bizarre situations, then either someone wound up dead or it finally finished and everyone went on to other assignments. You don't cross a jungle with someone and then call him up months later for a game of cards.

He had been good at it, though. Although the spy-drama aspect of it had worn off long ago and the moral questions grew more convoluted as he became more aware of the workings of his government, Alex had not seriously thought about other lines of work. But then after this last stint, Alex had had something of a breakdown.

For two years he had been posing as an Argentinian mercenary, running guns and drugs throughout Central America while keeping an eye on area subversives. Although the project had been instigated by the CIA, Alex had been a free agent for eight years by then. He was able to maintain autonomy simply because there were few people around as good at doing whatever needed to be done.

When two DEA agents were captured in Colombia, he was asked to rescue them. He got in all right, but one of the agents, already broken down by torture, unwittingly exposed him. Alex was caught, and his captors, soon realizing they had a most valuable American agent, took particular efforts with him.

The sort of guy employed on the torture squad usually isn't much for intelligence and creativity, so it took a couple of months of routine torture and a visiting "expert" from El Salvador for them to realize that their methods weren't working. The expert found the weak spot quickly. "You can't break a man like that with your stupid beatings," he pointed out scornfully. Soon, instead of hanging Alex by his elbows or holding his head underwater for near-drownings, they made him watch.

The Salvadoran tied him to a chair while they tortured the other two agents and forced him to watch as each was finally killed. He drove Alex to a village in the hills, and when Alex wouldn't tell him anything, he had it burned down. Then one night he brought in a peasant girl of twelve or thirteen and made Alex a final offer. "You can tell us everything and have the girl or continue your silence and they will have her," he said with sinister genteelness, waving with a sweeping gesture to the four thugs.

Alex felt the desperate panic rising again and shook his head to try to clear the memories. It was suddenly hot and airless in the office, and he yanked open a window, leaning out into the muggy evening. He would never know. There was the bitterest irony. For there was no nobility on his part, no selfless commitment to protecting others. Alex liked to think that he would have held up under his own physical pain at least, but he would never really know.

"I simply had nothing to give them," he whispered to the indifferent night. Alex was a lone operator. His handlers told him what they were interested in, and he passed along information. He never asked or was told about any other agents, operations, or plans. Well before they killed the first agent, Alex had told them everything he had passed on to U.S. officials, but little of that was news to them. He had information on guerrilla groups that, while valuable to U.S. intelligence, was hardly news to the local drug empires. As far as U.S. plans or Agency activities, he honestly knew nothing.

The men slammed the girl on a table, held Alex down in a chair, and forced him to watch as they raped her. If he closed his eyes or turned his head, they choked the girl until he watched again. It was only then that the Salvadoran finally realized the truth. In his rage and frustration, he began to beat wildly at Alex. They fell to the floor, and Alex grabbed the man's pistol. He shot his captors, took their plane, and flew to Miami.

After physical recovery, debriefing, and a round of "counseling" (How did you feel when they cut his fingers off and fed them to the dogs? Well, gosh, kind of bummed . . .) Alex was commended for his years of service and "retired" on disability. He disappeared, and was found, pretty much by accident, six months later cutting sugar cane with Jamaican migrant field workers in Louisiana.

That was all over now, anyway. He would learn to tap this mysterious stream of real life, find a few buddies, go fishing, watch the Super Bowl, have a magazine-ad life. He gathered his papers into a knapsack. He considered not riding home. He was stiff from last night's battle and his head throbbed when he bent over. Can't be going soft now, he chastised himself.

The office was quiet. A couple of officers were finishing paperwork; Melissa Barnes was still at her desk. She looked up as he passed, and he felt he had to say something, make some connection that would anchor him again in the here and now.

"Anything new on Morales?" he asked casually.

She shrugged. "They've got some bullets, nothing special. We figure the shooter had to be fairly close. There's a couple of possible spots they're looking at, but who knows? You heading out?"

"Yeah." He switched his helmet to his other hand and picked up a picture from Barnes's desk. "Your daughter?" he asked. Christ, he thought. Should I have been finding out stuff like this all along? Kids and pets and do you grow zucchini.

Barnes smiled. "Yes, she just turned nineteen."

"Is she in college?" It seemed the logical next question.

"Princeton," Barnes answered proudly.

"Wow, must be smart."

Barnes smiled and nodded as Alex handed the picture back. "Do you ride to work every day?"

"Sure, best part of the job." Alex laughed.

"Where do you live?"

"Coral Gables, just west of the golf course."

"You ride along Route 1? With all that traffic?"

"No, I usually go to Tamiami and take Granada south, or just scoot along on the grid."

"How long does it take?"

"Half hour or so. Depends on how hard I want to work."

"Hm—nice helmet."

Alex laughed and held it up so she could see better. It was painted with gold and silver spray paint, with now-tattered bits of grosgrain ribbon and reflector tape glued around the brim. She looked at it carefully.

"My sisters decorated it for a race."

"Do you wear anything else special? So many cars out, I'd hope you'd wear light colors."

"I have a reflecting vest—it's pretty visible. Don't worry about me." Alex slipped his knapsack on and left. Barnes turned back to her paperwork.

The cool fog that had carpeted Miami all day had by now absorbed the heat and fumes of the city, so it hung heavy, like a sponge of Miami's effluvia. The air felt like clay worked over all day long by too many kindergartners' hands. Every breath and sigh of the city was trapped in a soft, heavy cushion. Here was the exhaust of every car idling in the drive-through lanes of the fast-food kingdoms mixed with the steaming grease of the frying burgers; the bubble-gum exhalations and acne-ointment smells of the counter girls; the slow sigh of ketchup-stained wrappers as they decomposed in the landfills; the sweat of minorities in polyester uniforms, smelling of poverty and cooking oil. Here was the dog-straw smell of the greyhound tracks, the breath-mint-and-cigarette odor of businessmen, the mix of pheromones and perfumes careening out of the discos. It was as if the whole city were alive and breathing, sweating, smoking, coughing, spitting, pissing, laughing into the same sponge that settled in a choking blanket over the city.

Alex concentrated on the road, on the rhythm, turned on Granada Boulevard; only a couple of miles more. Traffic was light. Each car approached with a whine, was there and gone in a whir as he pedaled steadily along. Alex was tired and distracted; his head ached and the heavy air weighed on him. It took him longer than usual to realize that one car was nearby but not passing. He pulled over a little more. Usually, it would be some overcautious elderly driver who didn't want to rush past a cyclist. But still the car didn't pass.

He glanced over his shoulder at the car but saw only headlights, wide-spaced, probably a yank tank. Ordinarily, he wouldn't have worried, but ordinary events hadn't been much on his play list lately. A wave of apprehension slid down his spine. He decided to fall back and let the car pass or turn off. But as Alex turned his eyes back to the road, he realized in an instant that he was in trouble again.

One slightly slow response, one small carelessness. Alex was on an old overpass, a bridge with no shoulder and no escape. He heard the sudden acceleration and, in the twisted slow-time of danger, felt a wave of heat push against him, squeezed by the advancing car, a small push of heat, then the slam of metal against his rear wheel. Quick and agile, Alex reacted like a leopard, springing off the bike at the moment of impact and hurling himself toward the car to avoid being pinned or pushed off the bridge.

He hit the hood, felt himself sliding across the massive expanse of metal, a slab of metal, wide as a skating rink. It was a big car, an Impala, a Chevy, maybe a Lincoln; cars like they used to make, cars like hotel lobbies. Shit, he thought as he bounced across the endless hood. Where's a Yugo when you need it?

He slid across the mile-wide hood, bounced against the windshield, felt a sharp scrape across his back as the wiper caught in his jersey and snapped off, then tumbled off the other side onto the road as the car sped away.

Alex rolled a couple more times, got to his feet, and stumbled across the other lane, collapsing against the balustrade, his heart pounding. His chin hurt where the strap of his helmet had yanked, and he had bitten his tongue. He watched the taillights vanish around a corner, couldn't see the plates in the dim light, saw color only as a muted shade of gray or green. Alex coughed and spit out the blood, unstrapped his helmet and, when his legs had steadied, walked across the road to examine his bicycle.

A car slowed and stopped. "Shit, man! Are you all right?" He gave Alex a ride home. The car was full of dogs. Eight Pekingese, snow-white and perfectly groomed, with different-colored ribbons tying their locks out of eight grumpy little faces. They wedged his bike in the trunk, tying the lid down with a dog leash. Alex slid in. It's a hallucination; I've had a knock on the head and it's a hallucination. The dogs scampered onto his lap, poking their squashed mugs in his face; little wet tongues batted his skin.

". . . so we're halfway done filming this new Princess Puppy Palace commercial and the trainer she just—bam—falls over! Has a heart attack right on the set. So what the hell do I do with eight mutts, huh! I tell you, it's something in the air. This whole day been off—ya know what I mean?"

Alex wheeled the crippled bicycle into the garage and walked into his house. He flicked the light switch and stood for a moment, startled by the sight of himself in the hall mirror, covered with blood and dirt. He slid down along the wall and sat on the doormat, exhausted. He tried to remember that long ago this morning, for a few minutes he had felt good. Now, his favorite bicycle was smashed, his friend was probably a crook, the woman he was falling in love with would just as soon harpoon him, and dog hairs were stuck to his skin.

Chapter 19

Wednesday nights, Alton Torrance's wife played bridge and Torrance counted his money. He had never touched it, never seen it, thought of it only occasionally and then more by volume than amount. It was amusing to think of how it might look in piles in his living room, stacked on the sofa, on the coffee table, or on the floor, like Christmas presents around the potted palm. He liked to measure his wealth in cubic feet.

He had no personal use for the fortune. In all these years, he had spent only occasional modest sums, and then never for himself. There were cars for his children upon graduation and a gold bracelet for Emma once, but that was like picking a handful of cherries from a whole orchard. To him the money was peripheral. He looked with disdain on Roscoe and the other officers who took petty bribes and spent their money on frivolities like fancy boats and expensive vacations. Torrance saw himself as an ascetic, a holy man with a higher calling.

Still, he liked having it and he liked to think about it. Perhaps he would have done the same even without taking the money, but it added a pleasant dimension. He toyed with bequeathals and trust funds, imagined crippled children's homes and cures for cancer. But more than that he liked to think about how he would someday be remembered. He played with the headlines that would flood the media after his death, when his true life was finally revealed. There were great issues involved. There would be debates raging on the talk shows: "Hero or Villian?" But ultimately he knew he would be embraced as the man brave enough to *do* something about crime.

He knew what people thought of him. He was mediocre. He was competent, adequate, and unobjectionable. He was a small, square man, balding, dull. He had no illusions about his life. Torrance had worked his way up in the department through diligent work, attention to detail, and the ability to run things efficiently while offending as few people as possible. He knew the secrets to bureaucratic success. During his early days on the force, he had proven himself a level-headed, dependable but undistinguished officer. What he had since proven to himself must remain a secret to the grave. He smiled again at that thought.

Tonight, though, he didn't have time to play with his dreams; he had to solve the problem of Judge Selby. Now, there was a despicable man, a man of no morals and no consequence. His motives were greed and his impetus a kind of lackluster bravado. They had been partners of sorts for eleven years now; their system was steady and effective. It was the judge's idea originally. A major bribe offer had come his way just when he was in need of one and he had needed Torrance's help to arrange things.

John Keatson, an important Miami banker, was about to be indicted on money-laundering charges. He mentioned to the judge that he would be willing to pay handsomely to have some evidence disappear. Torrance had been a lieutenant at the time and in charge of the case. Torrance remembered the feeling of shock and outrage when the judge suggested it. If nothing else, he was an honest man.

And now I'm a more honest man, Torrance thought. Selby had finally pressured Torrance into joining the scheme. It wasn't all that difficult; he had simply invited Torrance out to his beach house and given him two potential scenarios for his career future. At the time, Torrance was just beginning to acquire the possessions and securities of home and family and eventual pension.

The major evidence against Keatson disappeared. With his team of lawyers, he plea-bargained to some minor financial indiscretions, and after a minimal fine and suspended sentence, he was ready to move on into new and innovative ways to betray the public trust. He probably would have been a star player in the S & L scandals of the late 1980s, if only he had lived that long.

As the story faded from the news, Torrance's immediate terror that his own crime would be exposed also began to fade. It was then replaced by guilt. The guilt festered and grew into anger, an indignant, righteous sort of anger that grows when one feels wronged. Torrance was angry at the judge for forcing him into it, but he downright hated John Keatson. The judge was just a greedy, manipulative man, but it was Keatson who had started the whole thing. He began to wish the man would die, and pictured him having a car wreck or heart attack. Torrance began to follow Keatson. He became obsessed with the man and found himself thinking of more and more ways to have him die.

The feeling was a sort of passion, and this surprised Torrance. It was a primal, epic lust for revenge. In his level head he knew he couldn't kill a man in cold blood, but as his obsession grew, he felt it would be a far worse crime to let him live. One night Torrance was sitting in his parked car across the street from Keatson's home, watching. The banker had just returned from a party. Torrance watched as lights moved throughout the house. He knew the man's whole routine by now; he had watched it many times. Torrance had not gone there that night with the intention to kill Keatson, but sheer luck set things off.

Torrance saw something suspicious going on in the house next door and suspected a burglary in progress. He radioed for backup. Two squad cars arrived within minutes. Torrance and the other officers surrounded the house, turned on the spotlights, and broadcast a warning to the intruders.

Keatson came to the window to see what was going on. That moment changed Torrance's life. There was the man who had ruined him, still in his tux, silhouetted against the window of his comfortable home. For the first time he looked exposed and vulnerable. Torrance didn't have to think. One of the burglars had a gun, and shots were fired. Torrance pulled his service revolver. His heart jumped; the adrenaline surged through him. He joined the other officers in returning fire, but Torrance aimed high.

The guilt was gone, but more importantly, Torrance had felt a passion, an almost religious calling. For days he walked around with his senses alive, a thrill with himself that he hadn't experienced since boyhood triumphs and first-time sex. The next time Selby came to him for help, Torrance was happy to get involved. That one had been easy: a drug smuggler, $50,000 apiece, then two months later the man was found dead in a classic gangland-style execution.

Most of their "business" was with drug dealers, but after a while, murdering them got to be a little boring. Violent death was not uncommon in their profession, and it left Torrance with relatively little challenge. He liked the more creative touches. A child pornographer had been blown up with a misdelivered mail bomb. After careful investigation, the bomb was finally attributed to a radical survivalist group that had been targeting an antigun lobbying group that happened to have an office next door. No one in the intended office was hurt; the bomb had exploded during the night, when the only one around was the unfortunate man next door. His dismembered hand was found still grasping a paste-up sheet covered with photos of small naked children.

An embezzler, liberated on a procedural issue, died in a boating accident. An arsonist, who never went to trial because of mishandled evidence, died some weeks later in a warehouse fire he appeard to have set himself. When the poisoned-Tylenol scare was going around in the early eighties, Torrance had been tempted to use it to kill his next victim but he decided it was déclassé and went for botulism instead. He had felt some pangs of remorse over that one, since it looked like the deadly toxin came from a jar of green beans the guy's grandmother had canned and the poor old lady had nearly died of guilt.

A particularly satisfying murder was currently in the last stages. The man was a rapist, but a wealthy, powerful real-estate-developer rapist, and his victim was his Nicaraguan housekeeper. Judge Selby had chastised Torrance for being so stupid as to fail to prevent the man's arrest in the first place, then intervened effectively before he ever went to trial.

The developer was driving alone one night shortly after his release when his brakes failed and his car crashed. He was not badly hurt, but he required surgery. When he developed AIDS sometime later, it was thought to be from a contaminated blood transfusion. No one ever considered that a police officer, who happened to be driving behind the man when the "accident" occurred and who stopped to help him, may have injected the man directly with a syringeful of the AIDS virus.

The only one who could possibly have seen some pattern emerging over the years was Judge Selby, but once he had his payoff, he usually forgot the entire affair. It was really Captain Torrance who had enabled it to go on this long. It was his steady advice, his cautious suggestions and ability to alter evidence as needed to diffuse the blame that proved so effective. Still, it was an uneasy partnership. Lately, there was too much talk about his leniency. Selby was greedy; and more important, he was stupid.

While Torrance always looked scornfully on Selby's flagrant spending, Selby had given little thought to Torrance's more austere life-style. Now and then he wondered why Torrance continued to live so modestly, but he brushed it off as lack of imagination. Selby had spent his profits on fat living and gambling and now found himself, troubled by ill health and impending retirement, facing the prospect of living solely on a judge's pension. Several months ago he had casually questioned Torrance about what he had done with his profits. He had mentioned it a few more times since then. Recently, the judge had suggested that Torrance might like to consider an "investment partnership" with him.

It must be urgent now, Torrance thought as he glanced at the clock. Quarter to seven; time to start the coals. The judge was coming over at seven-thirty. Torrance went to the garage and opened the old fridge. It didn't work very well. Usually, they just kept it for soft drinks and beer, but now the shelves held several pounds of mahi mahi and Hawaiian albacore tuna, purchased over the past few days from a variety of markets. As the charcoal burned down on the patio grill, Torrance sliced bits off each fish, quickly sautéed them, and tasted each one. Finally, at the sixth fish he found what he was looking for. He smiled with satisfaction. He cut two steaks from that fish, then took all the other samples outside and dropped them into the storm sewer. Always have a plan B, he congratulated himself.

Chapter 20

The judge arrived promptly at seven-thirty. "Alton, good to see you. How're you doing? You look great, just great. How's Emma?" Selby didn't look so great. He looked flabbier than usual, pale and nervous. "Really sorry we couldn't play this afternoon. Some strange weather, huh?"

The two men went out to the patio.

"Scotch okay?"

"Yeah. Just one, though. The blood pressure, you know. Damn doctors—have me on carrot juice and bran if they could. Now its oat bran no less. Oh, but eggs have less cholesterol than they thought! Whoopie. Can't even keep track of all this health stuff!"

"Well, I put some nice tuna steaks on the grill, and you know they're good for you." Torrance smiled indulgently. "Here, sit down." He slid the fish onto the plates.

Selby nodded absently and took a bite. "Um—good. Kind of peppery."

"I marinated them a little first. Jalapeño and grapefruit juice," Torrance explained as he took a big bite of his own fish. It tasted pretty sharp. "Is it too spicy?"

"No—it's great. Hey, remember you're talking to Mr. Tabasco here!"

"Oh sure, of course, I forgot." This was so easy, this one last performance of good ol' boy chumminess.

Tonight, however, even Judge Selby, who was so professional at chat that it had become second nature, was having trouble with it. He soon got to the point.

"The business I mentioned recently—we need to get things worked out."

Torrance nodded and let the judge continue.

"Something's going on—people are getting suspicious."

"Of you directly?"

Selby nodded. "Everybody—city hall, the department, too."

"Any talk of an actual investigation? Internal affairs?"

"Nothing yet, just mutters in the press. Some of the candidates are starting to blow the law-and-order horn and reel off stats on my sentencing record."

"That's normal muckraking. You went through two rounds of that already."

"I don't know, Alton, something's up. I can feel it. And some of your men are getting a little obvious. Weekends in the Bahamas? Can't you do something about that?"

"They'll topple. It happens. But they can't touch us."

"How do you know? How the hell can you be sure?"

"I'm smart. I know which cops are on the take and what their rackets are, how much evidence there is, and what it will take to keep them quiet. If there's an investigation, all they'll find out is that a few cops are taking bribes, which doesn't look great for the department but is hardly earthshaking."

The judge, generally a prime-rib man, had finished off his tuna. Alex saw that his face was beginning to flush, and he quickly ate a few more bites of his own dinner. He was beginning to feel hot himself, and a dull throb had started at the base of his skull.

"What about us?"

"Us?" Torrance replied, letting a hint of sarcasm slip into his voice. "What about us? Well, here I am a precinct captain with an undistinguished but adequate career and a modest life-style. I never take vacations, drive a four-year-old car, and have no expensive habits. I'm utterly average. No one in a hundred years would suspect I have the intelligence or guts to do what I've been doing the past eleven years." And you don't even know the half of it, Torrance thought smugly.

"I know how goddamn smart and sly you are, Alton. And I know what you think of me. Don't push it."

"I'm not saying a thing about you. It's your money. You live the way you want."

"But if I go down, you go, too."

"Which brings us, of course, to your investment partnership."

Judge Selby got up and seemed to stagger a little. He rubbed his temples. "Alton, I don't want this to get ugly. There's no need. I'm not asking for much. Can we go inside first? You have the air conditioner on? I'm suddenly awful hot."

"Are you okay?" Torrance feigned concern. There was, of course, always the chance that Selby might live through it, and Torrance wasn't about to risk his future with some premature gloating. They went into the living room. Selby sank onto the couch. Torrance turned the air conditioner to high.

"I know what you think of me. You don't owe me a thing. We split it all up fair. It's your money . . ." He was breathing hard. "You think I'm a stupid old fool . . . and maybe you're right. But I got to tell you—I've had a hell of a good time, and I'm not about to see it end. With all this new plumbing"—he tapped his chest proudly—"I could last another twenty years—and I'm not about to spend it in jail."

Torrance could see the pulse throbbing in the judge's temples. His breathing was labored. Torrance looked at his own face in the mirror. It was as red as the judge's. The poison was affecting him, too. His head felt as if it would explode.

"I promise you, it's only this once." The judge's words, droned on as if from far away, were dulled by the pounding in his ears. Even though Torrance knew what to expect, it was an unpleasant feeling.

"I give you my word," Selby continued hoarsely. "I just need to pay off these debts and have a little left for some honest investment. CDs or something, bonds, something safe . . ." The plea trailed off as the judge's voice grew strained. He pressed his palms against his temples. Torrance resisted the urge to sneer, restrained his contempt. He still had to play it out just right.

"Alton, I think I'm having a little trouble here. Can you get my pills? My head—it's like . . . oh God—am I having a stroke?"

He looked at Torrance with desperate panic in his eyes. "Help me!" he gasped.

When the judge stopped breathing, Torrance felt a rush of satisfaction and no small pride. It really had worked! He congratulated himself. He waited a few minutes. The hospital was six minutes away, and Torrance had to be sure a crackerjack paramedic wouldn't get to the judge in time to restart his heart.

He loosened the judge's clothes and laid him on the floor, to make it look as if he had attempted CPR. He spilled the nitro tablets out beside him and slipped one under the dead man's tongue, then called the ambulance.

The 911 operator heard a gasping, frantic voice saying something about food poisoning, then the receiver was dropped. She had to trace the call to get the address, which added another two minutes to dispatch time. Then the ambulance took seven minutes to arrive.

They found Captain Torrance, stricken and ill himself, trying to revive the judge. When they got to the emergency room and Chief Torrance mentioned the tuna, the sudden onset of the illness, and the pounding in his head, the doctor on duty recognized the signs right away. She gave him a shot of Benadryl. His symptoms miraculously began to ease.

"Scromboid poisoning," she explained to an intern as she took Torrance's blood pressure again. "We're seeing more of it these days. The scromboid fishes—mackerel, mahi mahi, and tuna, carry an indigenous skin fauna. It's common but harmless by itself. If the fish isn't properly refrigerated, though, these skin fauna start to produce a toxin. Cooking doesn't kill it, though usually there's a sharp metallic taste to the fish. Did you notice any strange taste, Mr. Torrance?"

"Oh God, I thought it was the marinade."

"Symptoms are usually immediate—severe headache, elevated BP, flushed face, breathing trouble. Most people don't have this severe a reaction. He must have eaten rather a lot. Still, fatality is extremely rare." She handed the intern a copy of the chart. "But Judge Selby had a history of hypertension, heart disease, arteriosclerosis, two bypasses; with preconditions like that, I'm not surprised." She flipped the chart closed and turned back to Torrance. "I'm sorry, Captain Torrance. There was nothing we could do."

Judge Selby's death made the eleven o'clock news, but after his hit-and-run dog-day, Alex was in no mood for war and pestilence and didn't watch. Rachel Brannet had missed it too but called him shortly after the *Miami Herald* hit her doorstep Friday morning. She had already hit up the FDA and CDC for information on scromboid poisoning.

"I don't see how he could have planned it, but if it really was an accident, it's awfully coincidental. And if it was murder, it's probably impossible to prove."

A slow sensation of horror crept over Alex. If it was murder—and he didn't believe in coincidence—this meant that Alton Torrance was a much more sinister figure than he could have imagined.

"Find out what else it could be, what would act like that—you know, artificial toxins or something, something a chemist could whip up. Call What's his name, that weird poison spook in Virginia . . ." he instructed.

"The one who did that crazy guide to home poison recipes?"

"Yeah. If he hasn't heard about this one, he'll be glad to know. Are they doing an autopsy?"

"I don't know yet, but I doubt it. The hospital says its pretty clear-cut, that this stuff is almost never fatal, but with Selby's condition it wasn't so unusual."

"I'll find out what I can at the station. Call you later."

Torrance, Alex thought as he hung up the phone. What else do you know? And what were you doing last night? He glanced back at the notes he had made from Rachel's information. Torrance and Selby were at the hospital by eight-thirty. That put Torrance out of the driver's seat. Murdering a judge was a pretty good alibi for not knocking off an agent. Then who had run him down?

Chapter 21

Alex got in late. The station was buzzing. Torrance looked tired and somewhat ill, but stoic. Mrs. James Beaufort was organizing a donation of flowers for the judge's funeral. The rubber plant got all of Alex's coffee after the first sip scalded his tongue. He said nothing about his accident. With a long-sleeved shirt covering the abrasions, there were no visible wounds. If anyone noticed that he moved a little slowly, that he didn't quite sit back against his chair (the windshield wiper had left a jagged cut across his lower back), nothing was said. Torrance shut himself up in the office doing some paperwork, then left at noon for a coroner's inquest, a formality.

At one o'clock, Melissa Barnes stopped by Alex's office.

"How's he doing?" She nodded her head toward Torrance's office.

"Okay, I guess. He's gone now."

"Bad stuff, huh? Remind me never to go to one of his cookouts."

Something must have shown on Alex's face, for Barnes amended her sarcasm.

"I'm not being crass. Torrance is a good guy. It must have been awful for him. But the judge was a pig."

"Did you know him?"

"Not personally. I testified in front of him a few times."

"He didn't seem to be well liked around here."

"You ever work your butt off for months on a case and then see the judge take a plea bargain and let the creep off with a suspended sentence? You'd see them coming out of the courtroom: And what are you going to do now that you've been found guilty of nine counts of felony? I'm going to Disney World!"

Melissa leaned back, slipped her heels out of her loafers, and pulled out a pack of cigarettes: Gauloise, a sophisticated red-and-gold pack.

"Can I smoke in here? Do you mind?" He did mind, but he wanted to hear more.

"No, go ahead. I've heard talk," he continued. "Rumors, really, that Selby was on the take."

"There's been rumors. He's flamboyant—was flamboyant, I guess, huh. He lived well, liked to play the dogs. Yeah, there's been talk."

She smoked elegantly, holding the cigarette lightly and moving it gracefully to her lips, as if she were on a piazzo overlooking the Riviera. Her nails were impeccably manicured. Alex wondered why he hadn't noticed all this before. Barnes had a certain class about her.

"But there's been talk about everyone at one time or another," she continued. "Some crusading reporter needs his Watergate, finds a cop on the take, exposes a 'pattern of widespread corruption.' You know the scene." Alex nodded. He certainly did know the scene. Barnes stubbed out the cigarette and leaned forward.

"Anyway, we need to work out this fish bust. Roscoe and I just got back from the marina; nothing happening with Tessely and Turner. I don't think they even went out today."

"Where's Wonton? Wasn't he with you?"

She shook her head. "He's not coming in today." Alex hadn't seen Wonton since he left yesterday afternoon.

"I talked to your shark lady—what's her name, Detroit?"

"Chicago."

"Anyway, she's okay. Said everything's been calm."

"Where did you talk to her?" Alex was obviously alarmed.

"Don't worry. I'm not stupid." There was annoyance in her voice. "I was careful. Asked her about scuba lessons and waited until there was no one around."

"Did she say anything else?"

Barnes shrugged and shook her head. She glanced up at Alex as she leaned toward his desk.

"You need a good chiropractor?"

"Excuse me?"

"You're sitting funny. You pull a muscle or something?"

Alex tried to relax and look comfortable.

"It's nothing, a little tumble."

"I told you to be careful riding around at night." Alex just nodded.

Barnes slipped her shoes back on and glanced at her watch. "I'm expecting some answers on the stakeout hardware this afternoon. It looks like we can get a cigarette no problem, and there may be an old fishing trawler we can use to anchor out and hide behind. If you want a helicopter stand-by, you're going to have to really justify the cost. I figure three agents and me on the dock. Do you think that's enough?"

Alex nodded absently. The Osprey Reef stakeout was not at the top of his list this morning.

"It sounds good—thanks. I'll look it over. I'm hoping we won't need it for a while if at all. I still think there's other ways." Barnes left, and Alex looked over the front page of the paper, scanning the story on the tragic death of Judge Selby.

A few minutes after Barnes left, Mrs. James Beaufort knocked on his door.

"Detective Sanders, there was a call for you from Washington before you got in this morning," she announced excitedly. "A call from Washington! Don't you think that sounds so splendid? Well, actually, he said he was a friend of yours. A Mr. Finneaus Lincoln from the Environmental Protection Agency. I mentioned to him that for eight or nine years now I have donated regularly to the Nature Conservancy and that whale group—what's the one? Oh, you must know it if you have a friend in the EPA . . ."

"I'm sorry—what was the question?"

"On, no question—oh yes, Greensleeves, that's the one, the save-the-whale group."

"Greenpeace?"

"That's the one. Where they all still wear those pretty bandanna scarves."

Talking with Mrs. James Beaufort always left people a little dizzy. Alex tried to reroute her back to the subject.

"Oh yes, he just said you could call him as soon as possible at his office, and here is the number."

She walked away, and Alex dialed Finneaus.

"Hey, still cooking on your garbage-boat business?" His voice was cheery and robust.

"What do you have?"

"Not much. Two small cruise ships and four freighters were ticketed for illegal dumping last year, but the files don't show much else."

"That's okay. Can you give me names?"

Alex scribbled the names down and dragged out the earlier computer printouts even as he finished the conversation. As they discussed summer in D.C., the latest congressional sex scandal, and Mitten's health, Alex was cross-checking the cited vessels. Two of the ships, *Matilda* and *Seastar* were on his list.

"Finneaus, I wish I could talk, but you got me going here."

"Something fit? So hey, does this mean I've cracked a big case or what?"

"Or what, but I'll let you know how it all turns out. Thanks a lot."

Alex hung up and sorted through the sheets until he came up with the crew rosters for the two ships. *Matilda* was a freighter, operating now mostly as a garbage barge. It had been caught twice dumping hospital waste loads off the Keys. It had a crew of twelve; nothing much to go on. The *Seastar* was a 150-passenger cruise ship with a crew of forty. As he ran his finger down the list, he almost missed it in the T's: Joshua Turner, engineer. Don't get excited, he reminded himself. Turner's a common name. But still, Eli, Joshua, maybe prophets ran in the family. Could be something. He pulled the name.

Chapter 22

"Hey, mon, you run off steamin' furious and stay away two days. Is this the way of a mon crazy in love?" Umbi was sitting at the front gate with Albert when Alex got to the marina.

"What's love got to do with it?" Alex replied sourly.

"You two meant for each other, you know," Umbi continued, ignoring the remark. "An' too much crazy for anyone else anyway," he added under his breath. Alex had to smile at this as he continued on his way to Chicago's slip. "Hey, she ain't there," Umbi called after him. "She in the shop—lubricating," he added with an insolent inflection.

"Thanks," Alex replied, and almost laughed.

Chicago looked up from the workbench. The cold neon lamp cast a harsh glow on her hands. How fine and ladylike they seemed despite the bitten nails, roughened knuckles, and daubs of grease. She paused in her work, holding a burned-out solenoid as if it were a figurine.

They stood there for a minute, Alex back-lit in the doorway, Chicago's expression out of reach, both faceless in the shadows, each looking for a hint. Chicago gently set the switch down and wiped her hands on a rag. Alex stepped inside the little shed.

"Can we go for a walk?" he suggested.

They closed up the shop and walked silently along the pier to the end of the dock. There were remnants of an older pier staggered like fossil ribs across an inlet. The tide was out, and there were pelicans sitting in rows on the mud.

"I'm sorry about the other morning—"

"Don't," Chicago stopped him. "You were pissed off and so was I and so . . . we got mad." She shrugged. "It's no main event."

"I know that. I just didn't want it to end like that."

"What 'it?' " She glared at him, and Alex didn't know what to say. "Look, I'm trying to be a sensitive kind of guy here . . ."

"Well, don't," she broke in, turning away. Alex looked at the pelicans. They all sat facing the same way. Another small squadron sailed in, five of them in perfect formation. Now, that's an easy life, he thought. Just watch your wing man and follow the leader.

"Don't you get just a little tired of this rough bitch act?"

Chicago felt like she had been slapped. More horrifying, instead of feeling her usual blaze of anger in response, she had a sick feeling in her stomach. She felt tears springing to her eyes and couldn't stop them, and that only made her more frustrated and the feeling grew worse. She said nothing.

"Look, I just came by to tell you I've got a lead on a guy on a cruise ship that could be doing the drops. We might be able to nail him and work backward to Tessely and Turner from there." Alex tried to make it clearer. "That means we have a new strategy. You probably won't have to do anything."

"Tessely wants me along next Friday," she answered flatly.

"Well, you don't have to go now. Besides, we could never be ready by then. It's only a week."

"That's enough time. It's not a big deal." Now that she had herself under control, Chicago turned back and looked at him.

"Why do you want to get involved in this?" he finally asked

point-blank. "We can bust these guys some other way. They're dumb; they're bound to slip up."

Chicago shrugged. "If I tell you, it will sound dumb." She sat down on the dock and pulled her legs up, hugging her knees.

"Okay."

She looked at him sideways. "Totally dumb and stupid, and . . . idealistic." She said this as if it were a particularly terrible way to be.

"I like a little dumb idealism now and then."

Chicago unfolded herself again and dangled her legs over the edge, tapping the still water with her big toe, sending ripples through her reflection.

"When I'm on the water or underwater, I feel I'm in the most right place. I feel perfect—totally right, totally accepted. Everything down there is balanced. Everything fits perfectly. There's no malice. You know that? Nothing in the sea *hurts* any other creature. I mean, sure, they eat each other all the time, but that's not malice. That's just life. Even people—we're the foreign invaders, and they don't even hurt us. Hell, you have to step on or grab or stick your hand in something to get hurt. Stonefish, stingrays, moray eels, sea snakes, all those 'bad guys' you have to intrude on to get hurt." She tugged at her hair, frustrated at what she felt was an inability to explain. "Even sharks—who have the worst rap of all—don't just chase you down and attack you! I don't care what you think."

"I know. I believe you," Alex broke in, wanting her to continue.

"Fire coral—it's got a sting, but it's not like humans, who go out of their way to burn you. If you don't touch it, you don't get stung. And not only that—it's not like its sneaky or anything! It *tells* you it's there. It looks like it will sting, and if you touch it, it does. No malice."

They were silent for a minute, comfortably quiet in the turning light. Then Chicago went on.

"When I'm in the water, I think I'm being changed over, that the sea is coming into me, becoming me, like I'm being all refilled. The sea is my own personal world. It's always changing, always the same, and always just mine. But being just mine doesn't exclude anyone else." She laughed. "I guess that's sort of zen."

She looked out at the inlet. The tide was coming in and a pair of egrets waded elegantly in the shallows. Alex said nothing, unwilling to risk the wrong words, wanting her just to go on and on, and maybe he could find some of the peace she spoke of.

"Sailing," she finally continued in a wistful voice, "is a perfect motion. Water and wind, and you fit right in between. It's like being in the palm of the world. Even when it's awful, in big storms when I was scared and thought we would sink, there's something so good about the power that even if it did smash you down, I think it would be okay. But then finally the storm is over and the sea is calm again, forgiving, welcoming. When I was little and I was sad, I would go walk out on stones and lay my palm on top of the water."

She glanced at Alex, a suspicious, embarrassed, hopeful glance. He said nothing but pulled her close so she leaned against his knees and they watched the tide come in. "Those guys are . . . invaders." She stopped then. The air here was still and hot. Alex found a paper clip on the dock, absently gathered her hair, and braided it, fastening the end with the paper clip.

"So Tessely and Turner are messing up your ocean," he said. She nodded, the thick braid rubbing between his knees with an unanticipated erotic motion.

"They're parasites. They're shits. Not even big shits, not some glorious pile of shit like rhinoceros shit. They're little shits, little daubs of gecko shit, little dribs of Chihuahua diarrhea . . ."

Alex interrupted. "Wait. Don't do that."

"Do what?"

"You start showing this lovely gentle side, then you cancel it. Why do you do that?"

"Who are you now, Dr. Joyce Brothers?" she snapped, pulling away. Alex ignored the remark but held on to the braid.

"I know you're tough—you can fight off sharks and thugs and probably a battleship if you had to. I don't need that—I've seen tough."

"You don't like it, fine." She shrugged his hand off. "You don't have to like anything. Just arrest them Friday and get them the hell out of my ocean!"

"You're not ready for Friday." Alex was alarmed and realized, even as he said them, that his words were futile.

"Too fucking bad. I—"

"Hey." Alex interrupted, grabbed her arm, and forced her to look at him. "I know about Stephen." Chicago froze. "And I know about revenge," he added in a softer voice. "It makes a damn lousy motive and often gets you killed."

"What do you . . . how do you know?" she asked. Her voice was a careful monotone.

"How do I know?" Alex laughed. "I'm a spy, remember? I could find out what day you had your measles vaccination and what presents you got for your sixth birthday if I wanted to. I'm sorry. I'm not the most trusting person in the world. I wasn't going to get into this thing without knowing more about you."

"So . . ." Chicago almost whispered.

"I know he was a marine scientist, trained at Scripps, commercial diver for a while, worked for NOAA in Miami, researched deep-water ecosystems. I know his boat was shot up and exploded off the coast near Caracas. Probably drug runners, but no one was ever caught." He realized he was still squeezing her arm and loosened his grip, letting his hand rest lightly on the soft skin inside her elbow. "I'm sorry."

Chicago's eyes filled with tears, but there were again none of the other motions of crying. She felt some pain but mostly an enormous sense of relief, as if a big bird had flown out of her. She looked out over the bay, the pelicans all squatted down in bunches on the mud flats. Mosquitoes were starting to come out.

"They were doing bottom core samples," she explained quietly. "Pretty boring stuff, but they had a grant from some continental-drift foundation or something. I had an ear infection and couldn't dive." He could feel one small muscle in her arm contracting spasmodically. She kept her face half turned away, staring out at the darkening inlet.

"It was one of those fucking war-on-drugs phases up here, with all the bastards trying to look good on the evening news by showing how they were getting tough in South America. Everything was tense. Colombia was the worst, but we got a lot of heat in Venezuela, too. Everyone was on edge. They figure some drug runners thought the research boat was really the cops, under-cover." Her voice trailed off.

Alex said nothing, afraid to intrude, to say the wrong thing. He took her in his arms and they just sat for a while.

"I know I can't avenge Stephen's death," she said finally, a recovered confidence, a new openness in her voice. She turned and looked him in the eye, smiled. "These shits aren't anything like the guys who killed him. I don't know what I'm doing with all this. Maybe it's just time to do something and this is what came along. But now it's here and I've got to do it."

"Sort of like us, huh?"

"Yeah, sort of."

Chapter 23

It was Monday morning and everyone was grouchy. Wonton was grouchy because his three-year-old had been throwing up all night after eating a dish of the neighbor's cat food. Barnes was cross because the dry cleaners had lost the jacket to her favorite suit. To add insult to injury, the willowy young counter girl with the king-size attitude had pointed out, as she filled out a claim report, that Barnes was really too short and stocky for Chanel anyway.

Chicago was tense with the strain of trying to be polite in such an unfamiliar setting, and Alex was gloomy at having reality intrude again. They had just spent a remarkably peaceful weekend together. No objects had been hurled, no tempers excited, and the usual swearing that echoed forth from the *Tassia Far* as regularly as bells on an ice-cream truck was strangely absent. Alex had started a verbal gentrification program of sorts; every time Chicago came out with the *f* word, well, she had to do it.

By the second or third "reprimand," Chicago had pointed out that if his plan really meant to clean up her language, it had a pretty major flaw. "I think the idea is supposed to be *negative* reinforcement," she suggested as they lay tangled and hot in the rumpled forward berth late Sunday afternoon. It was difficult to switch back to the square-edged reality of Monday.

The only one in a really good mood was Captain Torrance. Sunday's paper had carried a particularly fruitful obituary. The deceased, a real estate developer noted for his success in developing a chain of mini marts throughout the state, was perhaps more widely remembered as the accused in a sensational rape case three years previously. The official cause of death was listed as an "extended illness." People were still sensitive about admitting AIDS.

Regardless of moods, however, there was business to decide. The meeting had been going on for over an hour.

"So Chicago and Tessely surface with the tanks and get them in the boat," Wonton summarized. "Then she goes right back down under and waits on the bottom. As soon as we see her back in the water, we come in. Alex and I have about three minutes from the trawler here to the site." Wonton pointed to a spot on the chart a scarce inch from the red triangle that now marked Osprey Reef.

"If it's calm," Alex broke in. "What if there's chop or a headwind? Weather reports give us westerly winds."

"So it's a few more minutes. Alex, we got a fast boat. This baby moves."

"Damnit, we have to know this! Three or ten minutes—that's a big difference! She's sitting on the bottom all this time. There's limits on that, you know. What if she runs out of air?"

Chicago put down the pencil she was using to doodle on the notepad. She wasn't used to the dynamics of a squad meeting. She felt a little intimidated. "Alex, I won't run out of air," she offered carefully.

"How do you know?" Barnes broke in.

Chicago shifted so she could see the woman. "I know how much I use," she explained. "With a full eighty, at that depth I can stay down there forever—except for bottom time limits."

Barnes looked even more confused. "Honey, the closest I've ever come to scuba diving is rinsing panty hose in the sink.

What's a full eighty? What's bottom time? What are you talking about?"

"Sorry. Scuba tanks come in different sizes: An eighty would hold eighty cubic feet of air; bottom time is the time you can safely spend at a certain depth without worrying about nitrogen absorption and decompression sickness—the bends. It's all worked out in a chart: The deeper you go, the less time you can spend there. If you dive to sixty feet, you can stay fifty-five minutes, but at a hundred feet you have only twenty minutes; at forty feet it's over two hours."

"So how do you know how much air you need? Is there a chart for that, too?"

"No, but you can sort of guestimate, based on exertion, water temperature, body size. And again it has to do with depth. The deeper you go, the less time your air lasts," she clarified. Chicago turned back to Alex. "Even if we knock off extra minutes for activity, I've still got plenty of time. The drop site is only fifty feet."

Alex broke in. "What if the coke winds up in the trench and you have to go deeper? What if the visibility is bad and you guys can't find the tanks for forty minutes? What if you drop one on the way up and have to retrieve it? You know this better than I do —five or ten minutes can make a big difference."

"What if? What if?" Chicago was getting a little impatient. "What if I just get in the boat and ride home with them like we planned in the first place and you just arrest them at the marina when we land. Why do we need all this racing to the rescue stuff at all?"

"She's got a point." Wonton pushed the chart aside. "Any way you look at it, it's gonna look suspicious, us riding in like that. Why won't they just throw the stuff back in?"

Torrance looked over the group. "Wonton, go over the first plan again. Let's see if we can shore it up, put in more backup."

Another hour of debate and plan A was set to go that Friday. Barnes and a team would be undercover at the marina, monitoring the radios. Wonton and Alex would anchor their speedboat behind a supposedly broken down fishing boat anchored an inconspicuous distance from Osprey Reef. A helicopter would be on call, able to get to the reef in ten or fifteen minutes. Chicago would do the dive, pick up the cocaine, and return to the marina with Tessely and Turner, where they would be arrested.

"Umbi doesn't know anything about it, does he?" Alex asked as he walked Chicago out to her truck.

"He knows something's going on, but I haven't told him anything. I want to keep him out of it." Alex nodded.

They reached the truck. Chicago pushed open the side window and reached inside to pull open the door handle. The truck was twenty years old and eight shades of blue, some of it looking suspiciously like house paint. It was just past noon and hot. They leaned against the door waiting for the cab to cool off.

"I'm sorry, Alex. I thought it would all be pretty straightforward. I didn't think about all this stuff—things that could go wrong."

"You know you can still change your mind. You don't have to do this."

"Yes, I do." She kissed him lightly. "I do. Look, I've got to go. I've got students waiting for their first open-water dive." She got in and Alex pushed the door shut. "I'll be home tonight," he said. "Give me a call if you think of anything . . . or anything. Maybe we can go out one night this week."

"Go out?" Chicago looked puzzled.

"Yeah, you know—go out."

"Like a date, you mean?" She started to laugh.

"Yeah, like a . . . like a what you just said. I mean, we don't have to just fight, dive, make passionate love, or punch bad guys all the time," Alex explained as if it were a novel idea to him, too. "We could, you know, just go out."

"Like a movie or something . . . kind of thing." She leaned on the steering wheel, amazed at the thought of them doing such a thing. Then she grinned. "Well, I'll check my calendar." The truck bucked into reverse and she waved out the window as she drove away.

Alex went back to his office and shut the door. It was a long afternoon, and he was restless. The only one who seemed content was the rubber plant. He thought of Chicago's scuba students just getting suited up, ready for their first dive. They would be nervous, excited, clumsy, bobbing around on the surface, descending awkwardly on lines, pinching their noses and trying to get their ears equalized. But then suddenly they'd be underwater, looking up for the first time at the far-off sky through a ceiling of water. They would feel that thrill, weightless and free for the first time in a new world. Did she swear at them, or was she gentle and encouraging, holding their hands and easing their timid fears? He couldn't guess.

Wonton stopped in.

"We'll need to leave around four A.M. to get in place before sunrise. If you want to come out to the house Thursday and spend the night, you're welcome."

"Yeah, that might be good." Alex nodded.

"Could do a little cookout." Wonton jerked his head toward the captain's office. "Got a great new recipe for tuna!"

Alex shot him a disapproving glance but had to chuckle to himself. It hadn't taken long for the jokes to erupt. It seemed Judge Selby wasn't high on anyone's hit parade.

Chapter 24

There was another meeting going on that Monday as well. George Tessely sat uncomfortably on the marble patio of Dominic Kalispel's seaside mansion, drinking coffee out of the thinnest china cup he had ever seen. Why, he could see sunlight right through it. He had managed a few sips but was terrified the frail cup would shatter under his grip.

Kalispel's men stood around the edge of the huge balcony like bronze statues. Kalispel himself handled the china with his usual perfect touch, returning cup to saucer with the most delicate tap. He wore a dark green silk robe and sunglasses. His hair was carefully swept back and lightly oiled, the V-shaped rows of re-plants unfortunately still visible. Tessely felt coarse but still a little smug. It was, after all, Kalispel who needed him at the moment. One wouldn't have known it from the conversation.

"To get right to the point, George," Kalispel began, putting a nasal pinch on the vowels of his name so it sounded almost like a teasing. "We were surprised and disappointed when you failed to make your pickup last Friday."

"I explained all that to your men." Tessely tried not to sound defensive. "After Morales got busted, we just weren't really sure it wasn't going to come back on us. We decided it would be prudent to wait a little." He didn't mention the worry about Chicago's interference or the fact that his asshole partner had gone off and gotten drunk the night before and didn't show up. "Anyway, we're certainly set to go this week. No problem. No problem at all."

"Good. I don't believe in problems." Kalispel finished his coffee and immediately Mr. Soulange, the tall, long-fingered one who had approached them at the club, stepped forward to pour more. Tessely smirked to himself. Talk about overkill. He wondered if Mr. Moray, the stubby steroid maniac, was allowed within reach of this china.

"I'm sure you understand that we are allowing you to participate as a matter of"—Tessely bristled, expecting him to say charity, and wondering how he should go about saving his honor and still leaving alive if he did—"professional courtesy," Kalispel finished smoothly.

"We are, of course, appreciative of a new supply route at the moment. I just want you to understand that an organization such as mine could easily function without you should you turn out to be more of an encumbrance than an asset."

Tessely said nothing. Kalispel rose, and Tessely stood up impulsively. Two of the guards tensed. Christ, he thought, they frisked me at the door. What the hell do they expect I'm going to do? "That will be all. We will be expecting results on Friday." Kalispel swept through the etched-glass doors into the house, and Mr. Moray led Tessely around the side to the front driveway where a car stood waiting to take him back.

Kalispel watched as he was driven away, then turned to his assistant. "What do you think, Soulange?"

"He's a little on the Cro-Magnon side, sir."

"And what does that incline you to think?"

"That we can't trust him not to do something stupid sooner or later."

"Very good. And how badly do we need his enterprise?"

Soulange hesitated. Kalispel didn't like to be told things weren't going well, but he always knew where the troubles were anyway, and if he thought you didn't, then you were slack. "His system is clever but not really novel. It's been done before but, as his is, usually on a small scale. The advantage is that he's found what seems to be a perfect spot. We don't have to worry about losing the merchandise in some coral or risk it drifting away or anything. If we can locate the spot, we can do without the pair of idiots."

Kalispel smiled. Soulange was relieved. He had answered right.

Chapter 25

Thursday evening, Umbi and Chicago sat on the deck of the *Tassia Far* with a mushroom-and-anchovy pizza between them.

"So when you gonna tell me what's up with you these days, sister?" Umbi asked out of the blue as he pulled a string of cheese from his chin.

"What's up with what?"

"You hanging with new friends."

Chicago looked at him closely. It was hard to keep any marina activity a secret from Umbi, and she had been surprised it had worked so far. "You jealous of my pet cop, fish breath?" she joked.

"Ain't Alex I referring to. It's the fathead and his stupid friend who hangs like a remora. You do no good with those two."

"Relax, Umbi, they're not friends," she stalled, trying to think which of the explanations she had considered would really be the best. It only had to hold up for one more day. "They just have a little work for me, regular stuff."

"Regular stuff got to do with Osprey Reef?"

Chicago glared at him over a piece of pizza.

"Hey, don't give me no evil eye! I ain't stupid," Umbi responded indignantly. "Since we go for the fish there and all what happened consequently, Osprey been high up in your brain. First one thing happen, then another. Suddenly you talkin' and investigatin', then you get beat up, then all of a sudden you buddy-buddy with these guys so low they make bilge smell good. So, excuse me, but I happen to think something goin' on." He finished this digest of suspicion with a shrug, as if to say he didn't really care.

Chicago didn't know what to tell him. They sat in silence for a few minutes. Finally, she simply asked, "So what do you think is going on?"

"Something to give them lots of money—something in that particular place—but it ain't queen angelfish or spotted eagle rays. Something to do with all them wrecks."

Chicago had a sudden inspiration, picked up another slice of pizza, and took a big bite. "Shit, Umbi, you think too good. I didn't say anything because I don't really know anything yet. Tessely says he heard some talk about a safe on one of the freighters that went down. He and Turner dove it a couple of times and found some stuff—old jewelry—worth a few thousand, but he thinks there's more. He wants me to help salvage the wreck. I don't really believe them, but they're paying me up front. I had to promise not to tell anyone."

She felt bad about lying to him but great about him believing it. By the time he left, she had sworn to cut him in if there really was any treasure, and Umbi walked down the dock seeing each reflected star as a gold doubloon.

The station was finally quiet. Alex glanced at the clock. It was nearly 7:30. There were a few detectives out on surveillance who were due in sometime soon, but he had a little time. Torrance's office was locked; that was no problem for Alex. A quick search turned up nothing, but he hadn't expected to find anything, really. He figured by now Torrance was either truly uninvolved or so clever there was no chance he would leave evidence around. Alex slipped out and quickly moved on.

Wonton shared space with three others at the end of the wing. Alex scanned the desk to be sure everything would look untouched, then quickly searched it drawer by drawer. He hated it. It made him feel slimy and mean. He shuffled through memos and papers, two long-overdue library books, one on kitchen remodeling, one on mythology. There were a toothbrush and a toy spider, an organ-donor card leaving everything; the only caveat, listed under *"special instructions:* "Don't mess up my tattoos."

There was a bent and leaky tube of super-glue, a corner that appeared to have been bitten out of *Green Eggs and Ham* (—em in a box, with a fox, and ham, Sam I am) with a phone number scribbled on it in green crayon, three ties, a broken pair of handcuffs, a set of glow-in-the-dark stickers from Frosted Flakes, dry-cleaning stubs, some dated from 1985, a Spanish-English dictionary. As he moved his way down the drawers, Alex felt worse and worse.

The bottom drawer was locked. Alex picked it easily and rummaged through piles of papers. He was ready to finish when his hand felt something hard. Alex lifted the papers, pulled out three magazines—*Ladies' Home Journal*—and found a gun. It was a standard-issue police revolver, .38 Smith & Wesson, standard about ten years ago, before they switched to the Glocks.

Alex checked the gun. He would have to send it to ballistics to be sure, but from reading the reports on the Morales shooting, he had more than a hunch that this was the gun that did it—that and three other shootings: Quentin Ariez in 1986, Toya Edmunds, and Rafael Pierce in 1988. All of them drug dealers who had been arrested through this precinct, released under Judge Selby's orders, and turned up dead a short time later. There were others, too. Nine in all that Rachel had put together, possibly more.

A couple of drownings; a hit-and-run; a "suicide"; various accidents—suspects whose deaths had not aroused much suspicion or investigation. There had been no reason to tie them all together before, no pattern, no suspect. Rachel had seen the pattern only recently, and quite by accident.

Alex heard someone coming, slipped the gun into his pocket, and slid the drawer shut. He knew Wonton didn't carry the piece regularly and that he wouldn't be in tomorrow morning anyway. It made sense—Torrance, Wonton, and Selby, a little troika of power, extorting bribes for releases, then justifying it by knocking off the suspects.

He tried to summon sympathy for Wonton at least—he had the kid to take care of—but there was no rush of compassion. The most he could muster was a neutral sort of chill. Could he manage to keep his suspicions hidden tonight—eating dinner with the man, sleeping in his guest room? Alex nudged the gun down in his pocket. Sure—no problem.

Chapter 26

"Will you quit it already!" Tessely snapped. "You're driving me up the wall! For Christ's sake, why don't you just go home and let me finish this."

Eli Turner was nervously unraveling the strands of an old piece of nylon rope, twisting each one halfway down, then snapping it off with an irritating twang. "George, I don't feel good about this."

"You don't have to feel good about it. Just do it."

"We shouldn't got involved with real criminals. Kalispel is too big for us. We can't trust him."

Tessely pulled one of the scuba tanks off the dock and slid it into the rack. "You ain't backing out now; you screw me now and you won't have to worry about Kalispel, 'cause I'll kill you myself. Do tomorrow and then get out if you want—just show Chicago the drop sites and she can take your place. At least then I'll know I've got a partner with balls."

Turner rippled visibly. "And that's another thing. How do we know we can trust her?"

"Since when did you get so big on trust?"

"She practically blackmailed us to cut her in."

"Don't worry, I can handle her."

"Like your retard goons handled her, huh, George? We'll get rid of her, you said, scare her off good. Ha."

"So, ain't that one of those wise old sayings: If you can't beat them, let them join?" Tessely turned away in case he couldn't control the smirk he felt creeping over his face. Eli, how did I ever get involved with you? Tessely thought disdainfully. The man was almost sniveling.

"Relax already. She's just another dead-end boat bum looking for a new hustle."

"What about Kalispel?"

"What about him?" Tessely snapped as he finished securing the tanks in the racks and slammed the lid down on the gearbox.

"How do you know we can trust him?"

"We can't. He's a crook."

"So where does that leave us, huh?"

"What are we, asshole? We're crooks, too! Listen to me." Tessely sat down next to the nervous man and yanked the frayed rope out of his hand. "Kalispel needs us as much as we need him. His supply routes are getting squeezed."

"But we don't need him," Turner insisted. "We were doing just fine with our little bit—this is just greed. We've got enough dough. Let's just get the hell out altogether. Let him have the whole toy store."

"You know the trouble with you? You got no initiative, no goal in life."

"Thank you, Mr. Lee Iacocca. Who you trying to kid? The only reason you're willing to go along with Kalispel is because you want to be a big, important son of a bitch. We got enough money. Whaddaya need this big-shot stuff for?"

"You want out, fine; next week you're out. Meanwhile, I need you tomorrow, so get out of my sight for a while. Just be back tonight so I don't have to worry about you chicken-shitting out on me in the morning. And don't get shitfaced," he hurled after him as Eli stalked away.

He finished the tie-down and looked over the boat. Satisfied that everything was shipshape and ready for the morning, he pulled a beer out of the fridge and sat down on his captain's chair. What's Kalispel got that I don't? he thought to himself. A little more experience; that's valuable. Connections; but I can cultivate those. Good help. Fine china. He snorted in disgust. But I can find that, too, once I'm rid of Eli and the girl.

Tessely looked over the row of scuba tanks, neatly lined up and carefully secured, and gave the closest a nudge with his toe. It was one of the red tanks. It wobbled ever so slightly, making a dull clank against the boat's rail. Red. What a fitting color. Red, like the color of a dead man's lips after breathing from a tank filled with carbon monoxide instead of air.

Alex coasted down the streets of Wonton's neighborhood. It was just getting dark, the time of day when all the lights are just coming on but few curtains are closed yet, so he could see into the houses. He saw heads arranged symmetrically around the blue light of TVs; women passing back and forth in front of kitchen windows, wrapping leftovers in plastic; two kids wrestling on a couch, pouncing on each other in front of the bay window until Dad swooped in to stop it . . . all just glimpses.

Wonton's house was an older bungalow with some disorganized but sincere attempts at landscaping and a round patch of dead grass in the front yard where Dusty's wading pool had sat until recently, when the child got his hands on a Phillips-head screwdriver and discovered the joy of punching holes in things. Wonton's van was parked in the driveway; a second car, an old Impala, sat like a great sleeping beast in the open garage. As Alex rode up alongside it and dismounted, a sudden chill ran down his spine.

He turned slowly, looking over his shoulder as if the car truly were a beast and could be roused by his glance. It was a big, broad car, a muddy greenish color. Alex paused and listened for sounds from the house. They probably hadn't heard him arrive. He slipped his bike headlamp off the handlebars and shined the beam across the hood. The car had suffered much abuse in its long life; the beast had dents like Noriega had pockmarks. No way to tell there. He looked closer, running his hands over the hood to see if any of the scratches had the crisp edges or still-peeling paint of a recent hit.

Then he noticed it—a few tiny flecks of gold paint on the chrome above the windshield, where his helmet had hit, and one windshield wiper, snapped in half.

Chicago couldn't sleep. She sat on deck watching the lights of Miami and listening to the soft rustle of life from other boats. Someone rattled the lid on a teapot and poured the dregs into the water; Sir Reginald, the cat of the *Good Ship Lollypop,* meowed some minor discontent and was coaxed inside with soft kissing sounds. Chicago walked out to her bowsprit and back to the stern a few times, went below and wandered back to her weaving room. She had just finished a piece and hadn't restrung the loom yet, hadn't really even thought about the new pattern or colors yet.

New patterns, new life; she couldn't remember being in dock so long. The *Tassia Far* was looking more like a frumpy old lady every day. She needed to be out in the sea with waves bashing against her hull and wind in her sails. Maybe soon, maybe soon, Chicago thought, daring, just a little, to imagine them sailing somewhere together when it was all over.

They might just start with the Caribbean, island-hop for a few months to get the boat working right, then maybe cruise down to Belize, do the Rio Dulce in Honduras, then through the Canal and across the Pacific. Right. She caught herself.

Shit—you don't even know him. And he'd probably spend the whole time being seasick.

Fog. Thick and white; dense as lard; chilling and damp; all-surrounding and all the more sinister for its silent beauty. The sea was flat, squashed still by the weight of the air. Their little boat bobbed gently. The sun rose through the fog, a faint gray band across an invisible horizon that made little difference, as if a sleeping gray cat had only shifted slightly and shown its white belly. Fog—how could they not have thought of this? Alex stared into the blankness. He could not see bow or stern of their boat, and somewhere out there in the blankness were Osprey Reef and Chicago: out of sight, out of reach. Wonton had vanished. He was here just a minute ago. Alex called and called, but there was no answer.

The cold fog slid down the back of his shirt and clung in a fine mist to the hair on his arms. Alex shivered and wiped it off as if it were a spiderweb. They were enshrouded, lost utterly in the fog. He shouted for Wonton again. The hell with Wonton; the hell with plans A and B. He had to do something.

He scrambled over the deck, found the radio, flicked the switch. It was dead. Alex decided to head to the reef—he couldn't see, but there had to be a compass somewhere. Why couldn't he find it? The boat was too big. It was a hundred feet long, four-masted, built of trees and adrift. Alex was lost. He raced over the huge ship, tripping on coiled ropes. There was a humming sound coming from the rigging, a steady, nerve-scraping sound. He finally found the compass, its glass bulb misted over by the fog. He wiped it with his shirtsleeve and saw the needle whirling like a roulette wheel.

Damn—he would sail without the compass, but where was the crew? The sails were unfurled and flapping uselessly; how could he sail it alone? A slow, fat wave rolled beneath the hull and

pushed him off balance. Alex reached to steady himself against
the mast but felt it crumble under his hand. The mast was dry and
rotten. Then he saw that the boat itself was dissolving; the
wooden rails were pitted away as if they were being devoured by
termites, the decks began to splinter, the hull was cracking. The
whole ship was dissolving like a sugar ornament. The ship was
made of sugar—white bricks of sugar, pressed kilos of cocaine
now dissolving in the sea, poisoning the water. In a panic Alex
sprang from the deck, leapt out as far as he could into the fog.

He hit the floor and woke with a gasp, shaking and drenched
in cold sweat. He leaned back on his elbow and drew a deep
breath, trying to still the nightmare, pounded the floor with his
hands; it was solid and dry. He lay back and gazed at the ceiling.
Damn! We didn't think about fog! He jumped up and pulled the
curtain aside. The night was clear, the few stars bright enough to
overcome the city's omnipresent glow. The air conditioner's normal hum had developed an urgent whine and the curtains rustled
with its breeze.

Alex felt a drip on his bare feet and saw that the air conditioner
was laboring and sweating. He switched it off and opened the
window. The night was hot and muggy but clear. He could see
across the yard, down the street, as far as he wanted—no fog at
all. It was quarter to three. He had slept about forty-five minutes.
He and Wonton had to be at the dock at 4 A.M. Might as well get
started.

Chapter 27

"I got plenty of tanks on board, honey. You don't need to bring that," Tessely said as she handed him her gear.

"Oh well, can't hurt to have another, since it's here anyway. Besides, it's fitted to my backpack just right."

"Hell,"—he grimaced as he looked at her scruffy gear—"why don't we just ditch this old thing altogether? You'll be able to go in style now. Eli, we've got a couple extra B.C.s, don't we?"

"Really," Chicago interrupted. "Thanks a lot, but I'm used to my own stuff. Maybe I'll get some new gear soon, but today I think I'll just use what I'm comfortable with."

Tessely looked unhappy but said nothing. She climbed on board. The boat still smelled new, like chemicals and showrooms. Tessely pushed up the throttle as they sped out of the bay on course for Osprey Reef.

Turner noticed the trawler first. He squinted through the binoculars at the vessel anchored in the distance. "Who the hell is that?" he muttered nervously.

Tessely was at the wheel, gazing over the side into the water looking for the bow of the sunken *Aspen,* which gave him his first reference to find the drop site. He glanced up and shifted to neutral, took the glasses, and gazed at the unexpected company.

"Fishing boat. I've seen it around. Do you know who's it is?" he asked Chicago, handing her the glasses.

"I've seen it. A trawler out of Charleston. *Rosey* or *Rose* something, *Miss Rosalie.* Belongs to an old boozer."

"What's he doing out there? Is he grounded?"

"He's got an anchor out," Chicago replied casually, handing the glasses back. She felt relieved. There was no evidence of the chase boat hidden on the other side. "My guess is he's just broke down. The tub's a hundred years old. I looked at the engine once, but it's got so many jerry-built parts I got lost."

"I don't like it," Turner protested. Tesseley ignored him and, shifting to forward, resumed his search for their spot. He followed the strip of darker water that marked the trench until they were over a large sandy ledge. A hundred yards out from this ledge the wreck of the iron-hulled freighter *Aspen* lay.

Eli dropped the anchor and waited to be sure it set, then signaled to Tessely. He cut the engine.

"All right, let's get wet!" He was nearly bubbling with enthusiasm as he began to set up Eli's equipment, quickly pulling one of the red tanks out of the rack and slipping the B.C. in place. Turner gazed out at the anchored fishing boat with lingering suspicion, then began to pull on his wet suit.

"Nervous?" he prodded Chicago as she suited up.

She shook her head. "Not with a big, strong man around to protect me. Besides," she added, "you probably look a little more appetizing to a shark."

"Relax," Tessely broke in, still with an irritatingly jolly tone in his voice. "That's what we've got the shark suits for."

"I still don't understand why there are so many here in the first place."

"Has to do with the trench, I guess, but I'm no marine biologist," Turner offered.

"Has to do more with tons of garbage, I'd guess." Tessely

laughed. "That's what gave us this whole idea in the first place. The *Seastar* was getting squeezed by creditors. They decided the six hundred seventy-five dollars a month on garbage hauling was an unnecessary expense, and some smart captain realized Osprey Reef was the perfect dump."

"Pretty clever." Chicago forced a smile. "And then you figured since it was such an easy spot to locate and since no one ever came out here, you might as well smuggle drugs."

"Seize the opportunities, I say."

"So where's the chain mail?"

Tessely pulled back the tarp that covered the shark suits.

Chicago was adjusting the strap on her mask. She spit into it and began to rub it around, to prevent fogging.

"Catch!" he shouted suddenly and tossed the suit toward Chicago, too hard and far to the left. The throw took her by surprise. She reached out one hand to grab it, but the heavy suit was ungainly and slipped through her fingers. It tumbled over the side and sank.

"Shit! Damn forgot how girls are." Chicago glared at him and a felt a nudge of fear that was quickly suppressed by anger. "Don't worry—Eli's still got his. Eli, why don't you just go down and fetch the suit for the lady."

Eli eyed him suspiciously.

"Don't want her to get chewed up by a big ol' shark just to help us out, do you? Come on, shake a leg—can't stay out here all day." He lifted Eli's tank onto the gunwale and steadied it as Eli slipped the straps on, pulled his mask into place, and checked his regulator.

"Just bring it here alongside. It must be straight under the boat."

Turner just nodded, put the mouthpiece in, glanced over his shoulder, and rolled off into the calm water.

*   *   *

Umbi wasn't asleep. His cap was pulled down to shade his eyes from the morning sun and he leaned back in the rickety straight chair against the filling-shed wall with his bare feet hooked around the rungs, but he was far from asleep. Something was up. He could smell cops a mile away and the air around the marina this morning was fragrant with their presence.

There were two dressed like fishermen having coffee at Jack's, one in an unmarked car just outside the gate—unmarked cars being, as they were, unmarked only to babies and nuns—and that lady cop pretending to be a visiting yachtie. The pretend fishermen were easy. Umbi recognized one from a bust in a video arcade one night. Detective Melissa Barnes might have had him fooled, except she moved around the boat a little too clumsily for someone who had just sailed in from Bermuda, as the roster stated.

So what's going on, he mused as he watched the otherwise normal morning pattern. He heard the footsteps of Jay Lance, the station owner, coming down the dock. He had a heavy walk that got heavier when he was grouchy, and he would of course be grouchy this morning because he had to open instead of Chicago. Umbi waited until he figured Jay was just about to kick his tipped chair out from under him, then sprang up and swept his cap off in greeting.

"Good morning, Mr. boss sir," Umbi greeted him brightly.

Lance grumbled something inaudible, fumbled with a huge set of keys, most of which were to padlocks that had long been missing, and unlocked the garage. He swept his hand back and forth searching for the light cord as he walked in, didn't hit it, proceeded anyway, heading with a singular intention into the dimly lit shed, the coffee maker his only goal.

A clatter and string of curses announced that he had found it and dropped it and desired help. Umbi went inside to help. When they heard a boat nearing the pumps, Lance was just stirring his third cube of sugar into the coffee and not yet ready to face the world.

"Take care of 'em, will you, boy?" he muttered with the sharp buzz of his hangover barely quelled.

"Sheeit—Lord, this some boat." Umbi whistled and hurried to service it. It was a thirty-five-foot custom-built motor yacht, sleek and black as a jaguar, ornate with extras from the radar dish to the swivel fishing chairs.

"You want a fill-up, mister?" he asked eagerly.

"Go ahead." The skipper nodded. Umbi climbed on board and started to pump the fuel. There were two other men on deck now, and he could hear others below. He craned his neck, hoping to see something of the interior, half expecting to see it all gold and silk and chandeliers. The men were all tanned and slim in the way that Umbi associated with rich people. It was an unmistakable look, a particularly Miami look. Their muscles seemed cultivated and carefully arranged. These bodies were not accidentally strong; they bore none of the sinewy knobs or stark muscularity of the laborer or the graceful bulk of the athlete. These bodies could have been designed by computer and exercised by proxy while the owner was in suspended animation. Their skin was too good, too smooth, as if it had been cold-pressed in olive oil.

"Both tanks, mister?" Umbi asked as the first filled.

"Yeah, go ahead."

"Where you headed?"

The man paused, with a how-dare-you-talk-to-me-in-that-familiar-a-tone expression, then answered curtly, "We're going to Bimini for the weekend."

"Nice place, I hear." The man did not respond. From the other side of the deck, Umbi could see they carried fishing gear and scuba equipment, including several serious pneumatic spear guns. Cheeezus! Umbi thought. They can slice through Moby Dick with one of them.

"Soulange, did you program the heading?" a voice called from below. The man moved to the entry and looked into the interior, blocking Umbi's view. "Yes, sir. Hit that button on the side. It'll display—"

"Damnit, I know which button to hit. I've checked that; it's giving me gibberish."

"Sam, finish up here. We must be dumping numbers again."

"Nice place, Bimini," Umbi offered conversationally. "So I hear, anyway." The shorter man, the one called Sam, leaned against the pilothouse and looked superior and bored.

"You need any oil? Some bait? Good day for fishing."

"Nothing."

"A guide?"

Sam laughed. "We've got ten thousand dollars' worth of navigational equipment down there. I doubt we need your guidance." Umbi peered down to where the men were still gathered around the screen.

"Yeah, I can see. Works good, huh? Where you say you going again? Kansas?"

"Just fill it and stuff it, kid."

Wow, you're a grumpy sort, Umbi thought. What did you do, sit on a cleat? Umbi was beginning to see he wasn't going to make any new friends. "Eighty-four ninety-one. We take all color plastic—green cards, gold cards, cards with holograms of little birds . . ."

Sam just laughed, reached into his pocket, and pulled out a small wad of money in a gold clip, peeled off a hundred-dollar bill, and handed it over.

"There it goes," Umbi heard from below. "You had it on sat scan, idiot. This switch has to be up. Give me the coordinates and let's get on the way."

"Keep the change."

"Seventy-nine degrees forty minutes; then twenty-six-thirty-five," Umbi overheard as he jumped back on the dock.

"Hey thanks, mon—yeah."

The man called Sam untied the mooring lines and the other one came back up, took the wheel, and steered the boat away. Something all-over strange here, Umbi thought. They going for a weekend to Bimini in a killer boat with no ladies? Don't seem like much sense that way. As they edged away from the dock, the man belonging to the fourth voice appeared on deck. His face was familiar. Dark tan, heavy-set, thick-chested. He had long black hair combed straight back and oiled down, hair that originated in neat rows at the front of his scalp. The plugs were long since healed but still noticeable; they were too symmetrical—like a little garden—and came to a *V* in front.

He recognized the man from a newspaper picture; it was Dominic Kalispel. With a start, Umbi realized what else was strange. The coordinates he had overheard—they weren't for Bimini. They were dead center over Osprey Reef.

Chapter 28

Chicago watched as Eli Turner swam down through the clear water.

"The tanks are usually pretty easy to find," Tessely explained in the same breezy tone. "Once I find the *Aspen,* you just use that for a reference: about fifty kicks straight off her bow. It's a big patch of sand. They'll be there someplace."

She nodded. "You might as well get suited up," he prompted.

"But I need the shark suit first."

"Well, if you want it, you'd better go get it yourself." His voice had taken on a new edge. "Turner's not coming up."

"What do you mean?" She looked back at the water. It was still except for the ripples from their bobbing boat. There were no bubbles. "What did you do to him?"

"Filled his tank from the wrong end of a truck." Tessely smiled. "Get in." She glared at him. "Go on, we don't have all day."

"And if I don't?"

"Do you really need an answer?"

"What about the sharks?"

"They shouldn't bother you. You got here too early last time. They get pretty excited when the garbage is dumped—I guess it's something of a frenzy. But it's been hours now. There'll probably be a few around, but I'm sure you can handle them."

Tessely stepped over her feet and picked up a coil of rope in the stern. He cleated off one end, then threw the other, which held several clip hooks, into the water.

"This line's twenty feet long, so you don't have to surface all the way with every package. Just swim them up halfway and clip them on."

"I'm sure I can carry both up at once, thanks just the same."

"Getting snippy all of a sudden, aren't we?" He smirked. "The operation is expanding, sweetheart. You'll find ten tanks down there today."

Chicago took a deep breath and tried to calm the rising fear.

"So what's it gonna be—A) you get your ass underwater and bring them up; or B) I shoot you now."

"I guess there's no C) none of the above."

Tessely pulled a pistol out of a cubbyhole. "Get in."

Chapter 29

"Can you see anything?" Wonton called from the cigarette boat below. Alex lay belly down on the deck of the trawler watching Osprey Reef through the binoculars.

"Turner's been down about five minutes, but Chicago's just getting in now. I don't know what's going on."

"Any signal?"

"What kind of signal?" Alex snapped. "She's gonna stand up and do semaphore?"

Wonton stayed quiet, turned the squelch knob on the radio one more time just to be sure it was still receiving. Things hadn't been working out exactly as he had hoped lately.

Umbi ran down the dock to the guest slips and found Barnes in the cockpit of the boat listening to the marine-band radio. Umbi could see the tiny wire running to the earpiece that kept her in communication with the other officers.

"Hey. I gotta talk with you, lady."

"Sorry, kid. I don't have any work for you . . ." Barnes started to brush him off.

"Ain't lookin' for no work, Ms. Police Lady," he answered with a hint of insolence. Her eyes squinted a little, but she didn't change her expression. Umbi continued rapidly.

"It's okay. You pretty convincing, believe me, but I know you got a bunch of cops all over here dis morning, so I think something goin' on. Only now I think more goin' on than you maybe know about."

"What are you talking about?"

"My friend Chicago be out to Osprey with dese men Tessely and Turner. Then I see police all over dis place waiting for somethin' to happen. So just now I find out a big boat of bad guys headed out there, too."

Barnes looked puzzled. "What bad guys?"

"Big drug people. The one man with the hair stuck in his bald head in little rows. I seen him in the newspaper one day when I was cleanin' fish. Picture of him at a party. Chicago say everybody knows he a big cocaine mon."

"Kalispel? Dominic Kalispel?"

"Dat's de name, yes! He got three men and they're going to Osprey Reef."

"How do you know?"

"I'm telling you, I heard them! They come in for gas, they tell me they going to Bimini for the weekend, but I hear the numbers and know they for Osprey."

"Are you sure?"

"Sure, yes. I sure. What's going on?"

"I don't know," she replied cautiously.

"You got some kind of trap on Chicago?" Umbi probed with a belligerent tone in his voice. "She in trouble with the cops? I tell you she never in a million years be mixed up with dese sort. She think she going to salvage some wrecks. You know the cop name of Alex? Ask him, he will tell you . . ."

"Hold on, calm down," Barnes interrupted. What to do now? she thought. This could ruin everything. Or maybe, she thought with sinister hope, maybe it could be just the chance I need. How interesting that Kalispel would think to go out there himself.

"Look, let me explain this." She thought quickly. "We are on a stakeout. You're right. But Chicago's helping us—we're not after her. Alex is part of the team. He and another officer are out in a speedboat near Osprey Reef right now."

"Oh, mon, dis don't sound good at all. You got to warn dem."

"Yeah . . ." She made no move.

"Well, go on—dere your radio."

Barnes shook her head slowly and tried to look deeply concerned. "I'll have to figure something out. Kalispel probably has his radio on. I can't just broadcast something like this. Everybody in the world will hear it." Besides, she was thinking with mounting glee, this could be a sweet opportunity. Alex would undoubtedly see Kalispel's boat coming in, and he and Wonton would come screaming to the rescue. Kalispel was sure to outarm them. What better way to take care of that pesky newcomer who was poking around where he didn't belong. What better way to dispose of someone who was coming awfully close to destroying everything she had worked for.

"Look, kid," Barnes told Umbi. "Why don't you go back to the shed, and I'll take care of this. I'll think of some way to get word to Alex. We've got all sorts of backup for this, and I promise you Chicago will be all right."

Umbi thought about this. It was clear she was trying to brush him off, but what could he do? Fire up Chicago's old skiff and race to the rescue himself? Reluctantly, Umbi left Barnes on her rented Morgan and returned to the marina dock. Jay Lance was dozing on the folding chair by the door. Umbi went inside and switched on the radio to listen.

Chapter 30

Chicago descended slowly through the clear water. The tranquillity of her beloved world for once failed to calm her. What to do now? She might just sit on the bottom and wait for help. In forty minutes Alex would know something was wrong and come in for the rescue. But meanwhile Tessely would see her bubbles from above. He would wonder what she was up to. He couldn't do anything about it. Or could he? How far could a bullet travel underwater? Would the water deflect it? Slow it down? Would he come down after her?

She looked around the barren area and saw Turner's body lying lifeless on the sand, the weight of the shark suit keeping it submerged. Little fish swam around it fearlessly, already darting in for quick nibbles, used to the abundance of garbage in the area.

Chicago thought about floating the body. All she had to do was inflate his B.C. Would Alex and Wonton be able to see that from their lookout? Maybe, but Tessely would probably just sink it again, and it would piss him off, besides.

A shark cruised by in the distance over the darker water of the trench. It did not seem interested in the body. Wearing a full wet suit and all that metal, Turner's carcass wasn't exactly garnished for his plate.

Then her eye caught a glitter of color against the sand about a hundred feet away: the scuba tanks. Chicago felt a sudden resolve. This was what she was after—evidence. This was what she had come for. It was the only way to get Tessely now, and it was, in her mind anyway, some small way to avenge Stephen's death. No, she thought, revenge doesn't fix anything. But it can still feel damn good for the moment! Chicago checked her watch, glanced at her gauges, felt the buckle on her weight belt, all the automatic safety checks, and swam toward the tanks. There were ten tanks roped together. She untied them and picked up two. They were heavy, being weighted to keep them sunk and prevent them from drifting away. She could only manage two at a time.

"Thirty minutes." Alex put the binoculars down for a minute and rubbed his eyes. "And neither of them has surfaced even once."

"Maybe they're having trouble finding the tanks."

Alex shook his head. "It looks like Turner is pulling them up from a rope. Six so far. I don't like it."

"It makes sense, though," Wonton offered, "not to swim up to the surface every time."

"But with two people working, it shouldn't take this long. I don't like it." Alex slipped easily back down to the borrowed cigarette boat. "I'm going to call in."

"What for? They won't know anything."

Alex knew this but picked up the microphone and pressed the button. *"Snowbird, Snowbird, Snowbird,* this is *Miss Rosalie.* Over." He waited nearly a minute, then repeated the call. This time Barnes's voice crackled over the radio.

"Miss Rosalie, this is *Snowbird.* Go ahead."

Umbi jumped at the radio. He had been listening with growing concern for twenty minutes and had heard no sort of warning go out to Alex as Barnes had promised. He had been ready to go back and question her again, but now here was Alex himself calling in. Umbi was relieved to hear him.

"Snowbird, go to six-eight. Over."

"Switching to six-eight. Over." Umbi quickly switched from the call channel 16 to the new frequency.

"Snowbird," Alex continued. "We're still working on the engine out here, but it's been dead for thirty minutes. Just checking in with you guys. Over."

Barnes voice crackled in response. "Nothing much happening here. The crew is just waiting for your return. Over."

"Um—okay, no, uh, new ideas on what might be wrong with this old tub?" he persisted.

"Looks fine from our vantage," Barnes continued smoothly.

Umbi slammed his fist against the work table, sending screws and bolts flying.

"Okay then, we'll just keep tinkering and let you know when we're up and running. Over."

"That's fine. We'll be standing by on sixteen. Over."

Tell him! Warn him! Umbi slapped at the radio in futile protest. He picked up the microphone and was about to break in— but what should he say?

"Standing by on sixteen. *Miss Rosalie* out."

Something all wrong here, he thought. Something suspicious about that cop lady. Umbi paced the shed, stood in the doorway, and looked out in the direction of Osprey Reef. Was it just his natural distrust of authorities, police in particular, that made him doubt Barnes or was there really a problem? In Haiti everyone judged the feel of the spirit more than the words of the mouth. The feel of Barnes's spirit was not good. He had a sudden inspiration, went back inside, and picked up the microphone.

"*Miss Rosalie, Miss Rosalie, Miss Rosalie,* dis Coral Bay Marina. Come in, please."

Alex was startled to hear Umbi's voice and jumped to the radio again.

"This is *Miss Rosalie.* Go ahead."

"Yeah, mon. I just hear now you broke down. You want to switch de channel and we talk about it?"

Wonton and Alex glanced at each other. Alex switched back to 68.

"Yeah. Okay, mon, like I say, I'm at the marina and I hear of your troubles and I tink I can send you a mechanic out dere. Over." Umbi was affecting the strong accent and patois that he reserved for use when he wanted people to think him simple and nonthreatening. It was the speech he had used with Kalispel's crew, and in case they were listening now, they would recognize him only as the hustler who had pumped their gas.

"Uh, Coral Bay, I don't think we need any help right now. We're still trying to fix it ourselves. Over."

"Mon, you know dat's a good way to mess tings up! I tink you need help, mon. I tell you—I got expert mechanic can get dere fast. I got lot of mechanics wid no'tin' to do today but cause trouble. I can send you a whole bunch of 'em in a fast boat with a lot of tools. Fix you up no time. Over."

Wonton looked totally puzzled. Alex wasn't much clearer. Was Umbi really unaware of who he was talking to and just trying to hustle up a job?

"Coral Bay, I appreciate the offer, but no thanks. I think we can fix this ourselves. Please don't send anyone. Over."

"Well, you look the situation over good. Don't go screwin' no wires in the wrong place. You go putting amateurs in de delicate operation such as here and you find no end of trouble, you hear?"

"I'll remember that, Coral Bay, but I've got to get back to work now. *Rosalie* out."

"Right, my friend. I be standing by."

Alex switched the channel back and sat down puzzled.

"That was Umbi. I think he knew it was me."

"Does he know we're out here?"

"I don't think so. He's not supposed to know anything about this, but he must have been monitoring the radio. He came on right after Barnes. I think he was trying to warn us about something."

Alex leapt up, climbed back up to the deck of the fishing boat, and checked Osprey Reef. Tessely was still the only one in the boat. Forty minutes now. He scanned the horizon and saw, speeding toward the site, a fast black boat.

"Christ! Wonton, come look at this! We've got company."

Wonton climbed up on the trawler and grabbed the binoculars. "Shit!" He slowly lowered the glasses.

"A bunch of men in a fast boat with lots of tools."

"Whoever they are, they somehow don't look friendly." Wonton started back. "We'd better call the chopper in." Before he got his leg over the side, Alex grabbed him, pulled him back, spun him around, grabbed one wrist, and flipped him to the deck.

"What the hell!" Wonton shook his head and looked around as if he couldn't believe he was suddenly flat on his back. "What the friggin' hell was that for?"

"You tell me," Alex almost snarled. "What *is* going on? What do you know about this? Why didn't Barnes warn us?"

Wonton leapt to his feet with surprising agility for a man his size. A steady anger was beginning to replace the surprise on his face. Alex had his gun out and aimed at Wonton's broad chest.

"I don't know what the hell you're talking about, partner, but if you intend to shoot me, you better make your first shot a good one."

"Someone tried to kill me last week, ran me down on my bike. Yesterday night I found the car that did it parked in your driveway. Broken wiper blade and traces of paint from my helmet."

"The Impala? There's no way." Then slowly a pall of revelation spread over his face. "What day was it?"

"Thursday."

Wonton sat down, ignoring the gun, wrapped up now in his own suspicions.

"What *do* you know?" Alex prodded. "Is Barnes involved in something?"

"I drove the Impala three days last week when my van was in the shop. Thursday was the day my kid got sick. Ellen picked me up. Melissa drove the car home for me that night."

Alex lowered the gun. They were wasting time, but he wasn't about to do anything with a man he couldn't trust. "There's more," he said.

"Go on."

"Half the cocaine we seized from the fish market bust was stolen out of storage. The rest was cut to make up the bulk and returned. Only four people knew it was ninety-percent pure on the first lab report."

"You, me, Barnes, and the captain." Wonton's gaze was steady. "I'm waiting, Alex. You've got more than that, or you wouldn't be screwing around out here while your lady's about to meet up with one of the most brutal bastards in this hemisphere."

"Morales and three other drug dealers," Alex continued, "who were turned loose by our department later showed up dead. All from bullets traced to your gun."

Wonton looked genuinely shocked. "That's impossible. My gun is never out of my sight . . ."

"Not that one, your old one—the one you keep in the back of the bottom drawer, under three issues of *Ladies' Home Journal.*"

The confidence of an honest man, together with the easy nature of a big man who has never felt much need to prove himself, kept Wonton from losing his cool. He recognized now that there was a lot more to Alex Sanders than he had assumed and that it would take a lot more than he had at the moment to prove his innocence.

"I haven't a clue about that. It sounds like you're wrestling six 'gators in swamp in the dark. But from your point of view, I guess my hide looks like handbag material. I've got access, a weapon, circumstantial evidence . . . and a motive. My kid, right?" Wonton offered.

Alex nodded. "That about sums it up."

"What will it take to convince you that I'm straight?"

"I'm not sure."

"Why don't you think about it on the way," Wonton suggested. "When you figure it out, let me know, because right now we need to get our asses to Osprey."

Alex hesitated, then slipped his gun back into the holster. The two men jumped into the cigarette. Wonton took the wheel. The engine roared to life and, with a dramatic spray, they roared out from behind the anchored boat.

Chapter 31

As Chicago hauled the last two tanks up to the clip line, she heard a boat approaching. Shit, what now? she thought as she scanned the surface. Sound travels faster underwater, making it hard to tell exactly how close the boat was or from which direction it was coming. Was it Alex and Wonton speeding to the rescue? She looked at her watch. She had been under forty minutes. They shouldn't have done anything just yet. What was going on? As the boat approached, she could tell by the sound of the engine that it wasn't the cigarette.

Forty minutes. She had plenty of bottom time left for this depth, but only 1000 pounds of air. Stop, breathe, think, act: The litany for problem solving that she drilled into her scuba students now ran through her own mind. She held on to the line and took a deep breath. Okay. How much time do I have left? Another forty minutes at fifty feet. Can I hide somewhere? She looked around. The wrecked hull of the *Aspen* was the most logical choice—she could even hide her bubbles in there—but it was sitting in at least seventy feet.

Chicago reached into the pocket of her B.C. and found the tiny dive table she carried, made some quick calculations, and decided she could spend thirteen minutes at seventy feet with no risk of the bends. If she got to eighty, though, she had only seven minutes, and a scarce four minutes if she had to go down as far as ninety. If she overstayed, she would have to do a staged decompression. Not a big problem, except she probably wouldn't have enough air.

She felt a tug on the line, looked up, and saw the distorted face of Tessely leaning over the side trying to pull up the last two tanks. She let go and watched them rise. The approaching boat slowed to an idle, and she saw the shape of its hull overhead. Chicago's heart fell. It wasn't the right boat.

"Well, well, Mr. Tessely. So nice to see you again."

Tessely looked suspiciously at the unwelcome visitors. Kalispel's goons were adept at making their intentions plain with nothing more than a stance.

"I didn't expect to see you out here."

"You didn't. Well, there are some things one ought to expect in life."

Kalispel strolled to the edge and put one foot on his rail, looking down on Tessely. "Looks like you've had a very good catch this morning. I trust there was no trouble with the drop?"

"No, it was fine—nice and neat."

"Wonderful. That's just wonderful." Kalispel smiled. His teeth were a little too small for the rest of him—neat and rounded, prim little teeth that would better suit the runner-up in a rural teen-age beauty pageant.

"If you'll permit one of my men to board your vessel, we'll give you a hand in off-loading the merchandise."

"I don't understand," Tessely sputtered. "I was planning to bring it in myself."

Kalispel nodded to Moray and the man jumped down onto the smaller craft. He brushed past Tessely without a word and grabbed the nearest of the cocaine-filled tanks.

"Oh well, I guess this is easy as anything." Tessely laughed nervously. "Save me the trouble."

Kalispel laughed, a hearty, genuinely pleased laugh.

"That's very good, that's really very funny. Shows a bit of gumption and no small intelligence. Believe it or not, Mr. Tessely, some people in your situation would start protesting this whole thing. Your slightly obsequious demeanor and evident willingness to grovel may save your life."

The weighted tanks were heavy, and even the pumped and primed Mr. Moray had trouble handing them up and over to the other boat.

"Where's your partner?" Kalispel frowned. "The twitchy little fellow?"

"He's dead. He didn't want to get involved with you, and I was afraid he might talk," Tessely explained with all the boldness he could muster, hoping this foresight might endear him to this man, who quite clearly had come out here ready to kill him.

"Whose bubbles are those then?" Kalispel asked. If he was impressed by this action, he did not show it.

"Just a diver I picked up to replace Eli. This is her first time. She doesn't know anything about you. She's expendable."

The talk was interrupted by the roar of an engine. All heads turned in the direction of the anchored trawler as a spray of water sliced the horizon and a new boat roared toward them. Kalispel's men leapt to action, pulling out an assortment of weapons that made the hardware on *Miami Vice* look like something Julia Child would use to whip up a soufflé. Tessely pulled open the hutch by the helm and grabbed his own pistol, but Moray backhanded him with one swat that sent him flying.

Kalispel motioned to two of his men, pointing at the circle of bubbles in the water. "Get the girl."

The two men pulled their shirts off and tossed on the waiting scuba gear.

*　*　*

Chicago heard the splash, looked up, and saw the two figures silhouetted against the sky. She didn't know who they were, but when she saw the outline of their spear guns, she decided it wasn't Jacques Cousteau coming to film the beauty of the underwater world. Quickly, she dove for the shelter of the wreck.

"Shit—"

"What's going on?" Wonton shouted as he shoved the throttle to full.

"Kalispel just put two men in the water. He's got one on Tessely's boat, two on deck. Major firepower." Alex handed Wonton the binoculars and grabbed his scuba gear.

"How long for the chopper?"

"If they took off right away, another ten minutes."

"Go past on the port side," Alex shouted, "as close as you can. Drop me, then . . . I don't know. Try to distract them."

"Right. Maybe we can talk about the weather," Wonton replied vigorously. "Hand me the Hanky," he shouted, using his pet name for the HK submachine gun.

Alex gave him the gun, pulled his own out, and set it in the cubby beneath the wheel ready at hand, then pulled his fins on, strapped his tank on, and sat crouched on the side, ready to roll in.

"Hey, Wonton," he shouted as they neared the two boats and the first shots slammed into their hull. "What are you doing reading *Ladies' Home Journal*?"

Wonton ducked and fired back at Kalispel one-handed, the gun braced against his chest.

"They printed my wife's recipes!" he hollered as he swung in close, pulled the throttle down, shifted to neutral, fired a sweep of bullets over the immaculate deck of the drug dealer's boat, and screamed, *"Go!"*

Alex rolled off and hit the water, dropping immediately beneath the surface. Wonton paused for a second to make sure he had cleared the prop, then hit the gearshift back to forward and kicked the throttle up, spun the wheel to arc his boat away, and ducked for shelter as a renewed barrage of lead whistled over his head.

Chapter 32

The *Aspen* lay on her port side, nestled against the reef wall like some giant whale calf. The bow was tilted slightly up, as if she had tried valiantly to keep her nose out of water as she was sinking. Algae clung to her hull in streamers like a woman's hair. There was a current in the trench and a cold upswelling that left a thermocline right at the sunken ship's level, making the water look shimmery.

Wreck diving was a favorite pastime for many sport divers, but Chicago hated it. Freighters like this had been her home; the men who had died when the *Aspen* sank were men like her father and his crew. She could not bear to swim among the ruins of their lives. But now she had no choice. She swam quickly over the hull and scanned it for any possible hiding place. She peeked in one open doorway and was startled by a giant grouper, which, equally startled, retreated deeper into its sanctuary.

Finally, she found a long rip in the starboard bow where the misguided freighter had struck the sharp reef. There was enough room to hide and an open hatch nearby if she needed to escape. Quickly, Chicago slipped in and edged up into the bow where her bubbles would be trapped and not give her away.

*   *   *

Alex swam quickly to the bottom. From here, the surface war was nothing but noise and shadowy hulls. The hull of the cigarette skipped across the water, making circles around the larger shadow of Kalispel's boat. Tessely's vessel, still anchored, bobbed solidly above. Alex stopped to wrap Tessely's anchor chain a few times around a chunk of coral to prevent his easy escape. He offered a silent apology to the millions of coral polyps and thousands of years of reef development he had just destroyed by this, then swam toward the edge of the reef wall. He could see two columns of bubbles rising from the trench below. There ought to have been three.

Kalispel's two aquatic goons were searching the near side of the wrecked ship. One was skirting the tilted keel, looking under the hull, while the other stopped to peer in open hatches and portholes. They weren't in position to see what Alex could—tiny bubbles, like the kind that stream up out of the cracks in a child's rubber duck when dunked in the tub, leaking slowly out from rivet holes in the bow.

She's alive! he thought with relief. Alex waited until the two men had circled the stern and began to search the other side. Once below the tipped hull, they couldn't see him. Quickly, Alex dove down to the bow.

"Okay, sweetheart," he muttered into his regulator. "Let's see if you learned this on Daddy's boat." Gently, Alex tapped on the hull: dot dash: A; dot dash dot dot: L He waited. In just a second came the rapid reply—five letters: G-R-E-A-T. She somehow managed to sound sarcastic even in Morse code.

He glanced at his watch. Another five minutes at least until they could expect the helicopter with backup. They're going to know I'm here soon enough, he figured. I might as well introduce myself. Now, how did they used to do this on *Sea Hunt*? Keeping his body low against the silt-covered deck, Alex crept up over the edge of the *Aspen* and saw the two divers below. When the man in front swam through a gash in the hull, Alex tucked his arms in and dropped like a falcon on top of the man in the rear.

Chicago peered out the gash and glimpsed both thugs swimming toward her hiding place. While she was sort of hoping to see *Jaws* 1, 2, or 3 appear out of the deep and swallow them both, the attacking figure of Alex, diving like a torpedo, was equally welcome.

Sensing Alex's presence a moment before contact, the man turned. Alex grabbed his spear gun, but the moment was enough time to react, time enough to tighten his grip. The two men began to struggle.

The other diver didn't see the attack. He continued scanning the ripped hull, poking his head farther inside the jagged metal, letting his eyes adjust to the dim light. Chicago crouched as small as she could, trying to breathe silently, waiting until he got close enough. The pink man, she nicknamed him, for he wore, oddly enough, a bright bubble-gum-pink Tusa mask. Maybe he doubles as a model for *Skindiver,* she thought. Just come a little closer, she willed him. Suddenly, something brushed past her arm, long, soft, and silky, an eel disturbed from its nook. Startled, Chicago moved, sending up a little swirl of silt. The pink man saw it, realized she was close and, pulling his body half in the hole, drew the spear gun up.

Chicago lunged toward him and kicked hard. One heel landed square in his face, knocking his mask off and regulator out. She heard the *thwup* as the pneumatic spear gun was released and the clank as the point hit the metal hull. She pushed away and escaped through the hatch.

She looked around for Alex. He and the other diver were locked together, wrestling over the weapon, their bodies turning together in an oddly graceful underwater ballet. Alex, trained and experienced in hand-to-hand combat, thought like a fighter. Chicago, experienced in the infinite array of dumb things people could do underwater, thought like a scuba instructor.

As Alex struggled to break the man's grip, Chicago simply swam up from behind, straddled his tank with her knees, and yanked on his regulator hose with one hand while reaching around to grab his weight-belt buckle with the other. She pulled his mouthpiece out, and with one good yank on the quick-release buckle, the belt fell away. The diver let go of Alex, twisted free and, now unweighted, began to drift up. He lunged at Chicago. Alex grabbed the spear gun but dropped it as the man's foot caught him under the chin.

Chicago felt a strong grip on her ankle, then the man was pulling her toward him, hand over hand along her leg. She held his regulator over her head, like a child who has stolen another's toy and wants to taunt him. She kicked and pulled to escape his grip, but a man after air has rare strength and soon he had her in a clinch, clawing at her own regulator.

Then his head snapped back. Alex had him around the neck. Chicago wasn't through yet, either. She grabbed for the auto-inflator button and pumped his vest full of air. Alex got clued in quickly. Hearing the power inflator, he let go. Their attacker, now buoyant, zoomed skyward. Just for good measure, Alex yanked off one fin. With no weight belt and only one fin, he would have a difficult time getting back down to cause them any more trouble.

Their eyes met for the first time. Chicago's were bright with excitement and a little smugness. She was enjoying their victory; but she saw only alarm on Alex's face. The victory was brief. The pink man was swimming in from behind her, spear gun reset and ready. Alex grabbed Chicago and pushed her aside, kicking hard and twisting his body in front of hers. He was almost quick enough. Again Chicago heard the sickening sound of the pneu-

matic gun, then she felt her throat seize as she saw the spear hit
Alex.

The spear went straight through his upper arm and gashed the
side of his chest. Alex's body contorted with the pain. A dark
cloud of blood drifted into the water. Chicago felt the sour taste
of vomit in the back of her throat. The pink man dropped the
gun. This pulled the spear, still attached by the shock cord, back
through the wound. The spear point ripped a couple of inches of
flesh out of Alex's side as it was jerked back, then the toggle tip
caught on the back of his arm, preventing it from going any
further.

The pink man turned toward Chicago. She froze for a second.
Think! Think! She had to help Alex, but knew she couldn't
outfight this guy alone. If she could get him away, though, Alex
could get himself to the surface—she hoped. She turned and
kicked hard, glancing around to get her bearings. With a shock,
she realized that in the fighting they had drifted deep into the
trench. The wrecked *Aspen,* lying seventy feet deep, was far above
them. The shimmering thermocline spread like a film of gasoline
all around. She didn't have to look at her depth gauge; she knew
they had to be 140 or 150 feet down. The colder water was
denser; she was kicking as hard as she could and not ascending
very much.

Chicago pumped a short blast of air into her vest and felt
herself rise a little. She also felt the subtle hesitation in the auto-
inflater that told her she was getting low on air. She sighted the
bow of the wreck and swam up toward it, glancing back to check
on her pursuer. He was gaining fast. No plan now, she thought—
up, down, shit all over. I can get killed right here by the pink man
or shot by Tessely on the surface; I'm probably already fucking
bent. Maybe I'll just swim down the trench, get narced, and feed
the sharks. It's kind of like a salad bar of death.

She swam as hard as she could. The pink man, fresh and strong with a full tank of air, was gaining on her. Just then she saw a glint from the coral, a flash of silvery-gray, a flicker of fluorescent orange. The other spear gun, still cocked, lay where it had fallen, wedged between two lumps of brain coral. Glancing over her shoulder, she could see the pink man's face—large pores. Oh shit. With all the strength she had left, she kicked toward the gun. As she neared it, she felt a jerk on her fin. She tucked her knees, dropped down, and grabbed the gun. It was wedged tight.

Her body was jolted backward. The pink man had grabbed her tank valve like the scruff of a dog's neck and was trying to drag her up. Jamming one elbow between the coral heads in order to hold on, she tried to free the gun. The pink man responded by trying to ram her head through the coral. He shook her like a rag doll, up and down, for what seemed like minutes. Her face burned from being scraped against the coral. Her mask flooded with water, and she bit down hard on her mouthpiece to hold on to the regulator. She felt her arms weakening. Then suddenly she felt a new tug, then release. The man let go and she fell forward. The force knocked the spear gun free.

She pulled it to her side and slowly turned, hanging on to the coral, trying to clear her head. Through her flooded mask she could only see some tangled flurry of shapes and bubbles nearby and thought perhaps the sharks had attacked the pink man. Then she realized it was Alex. He had pulled the pink man off. Her hands shaking, Chicago pulled her mask back in place. Fumbling, she had trouble clearing and choked on the water. Finally, she could see. Alex was barely holding on. All he could do was stay on the pink man's back, holding on one-handed like he was riding a bull. His wounded arm hung limply. The spear was still stuck through the arm, but he had cut the shock cord, freeing the shaft from the gun. Blood was still flowing heavily from the wound, clouding the water. Chicago pulled her spear gun into place and swam closer. She had a clear shot: two feet away and the logo on his B.C. right over the heart.

Chicago had never speared a fish. She had tried a couple of times, but when it would come time to pull the trigger, she would always miss. Stephen used to tease her that she missed on purpose, and this was probably true. She had no idea how it felt when the spear struck, the slight tug as the cord jerked taut, the faint vibration of the impact traveling back along through the gun to her hand. The sound startled her; the solidness of the man's body surprised her. Hitting him squarely in the chest like that, it could have been a wall or tree trunk. She thought she could feel every contraction of muscle, every convulsive shiver vibrating down the metal shaft into her hand.

She dropped the gun as if it were electrified. The spear stuck out of the man's chest right below the sternum, between the buckles of his B.C. He clutched it with both hands, then relaxed. Alex let go. The pink man's body twitched a few times, then hung motionless, bent double. Slowly, he began to sink.

Chicago started to gag. She had just killed a man. She felt dizzy and heard a loud roar in her ears. It was getting hard to breathe. Her lungs were beginning to burn, but she couldn't remember what to do. She looked toward the surface, a faint blue hope a thousand miles away.

Then Alex was there. He grabbed her B.C., hooked one leg around hers to keep hold of her, then pushed his octopus against her face. She pulled out her now useless regulator and grabbed his. Air—what a beautiful taste. They hung there together for almost a minute, huddled together against the wall, limbs entwined, sharing air and life. Her head began to clear and she realized they were still in a bad situation.

She looked at Alex. His arm was bleeding badly and his body seemed too heavy. She put her palm to his chest, needing to know he was really alive, and felt his heartbeat, weak and fast, fluttery as that of a bird hit by a car. He pushed her hand away, tried to smile through his mask, and gave her an okay signal. She could tell he was lying. She looped her arm through his B.C. and slowly began to swim them up.

Far below, the sharks of Osprey Reef had sensed the excitement and smelled the blood. They swam up and soon found the pink man's bleeding body. Cautiously at first, they circled, backs arched, twitching excitedly at the scent of blood in the water. First one, then another, growing bolder, darting in for a quick bump, then finally a bite. A feeding frenzy erupted.

Chicago and Alex looked away. What could they do? A plume of blood trailed them as they made the long, slow ascent. A few of the sharks followed, whipped to anxiety by the boats droning on the surface, by the rhythmic throb of the helicopter hovering overhead, and by the blood. They circled closer. So much for a decompression stop, Chicago thought. The water was a lighter blue as they neared the surface. Forty feet, thirty, twenty.

Alex felt a shark bump his leg. He squeezed his eyes shut and reminded God that even if he himself wasn't banking with the Almighty, He might at least check his grandmother's account.

"I see 'em. I see 'em now!" Wonton's shouts were futile, for the chopper was too noisy, but the others had seen them, too. There were two police boats and a coast guard cutter on the scene. It had arrived, fortunately, just in time to scoop Wonton up off the last remaining planks of the shot-to-hell cigarette. Kalispel was in handcuffs. Soulange was disgusted. Mr. Moray, shot in six places, still needed restraints. Tessely was having some sort of weepy hysterics. The diver who Chicago and Alex had sent rushing to the surface had forgotten the most basic rule of diving, held his breath all the way up, and embolized.

Now everyone watched tensely as the figures of Alex and Chicago drifted into sight. First they could just see the colors, the orange of the B.C.s, the blue-and-yellow tanks, then they could see their outlines, then finally, the menacing sharks that accompanied them.

"Holy shit!"

They hit the surface at the stern of the cutter. Wonton leaned over and grabbed Chicago's tank as she clutched at the boat and pulled her aboard. Alex flung his good arm over the side and kicked hard, but the spear got caught on the hull and with a jolt of pain he fell back away from the boat. A fin broke the water. Everyone watched in horror as Alex was dragged under. Two officers began firing at the sharks. Without thinking, Wonton jumped in, feet first, landing, he only realized later, squarely on the head of a shark. He caught hold of Alex and shoved him back toward the boat. Chicago grabbed him, and Wonton boosted him into the boat, then wasted no time in his own ungraceful but swift entry.

The three lay gasping. Wonton wiped the water out of his eyes, then stared horrified at Alex's foot.

"Oh my God!" he whispered. Half the fin was gone, cleanly bitten away.

"Shit," Alex muttered. "Nicked my big toe." He started to laugh, a great heaving, water-spattered laugh that made him choke. Then a shudder went through his body. Wonton started to guffaw, his shoulders shaking with relief as he reached a hand toward Alex to help him up. Alex didn't move. Then Wonton saw the pool of blood.

"Whoa, buddy. What's with this? You okay?" His face turned suddenly serious. "What is this arrow shit? Hey, I need some help with this! He's shot!" he shouted at the captain, then turned quickly to Chicago. She was kneeling, watching in a panic-stricken silence while another coast guard officer pulled her tank off. "You hurt?" Wonton yelled. She shook her head.

Wonton turned back to Alex. His face had gone white and his

breathing was shallow. The blood had turned into a little river, flowing this way and that with the rocking of the boat, mixing with water and soaking into a life vest that lay nearby. Wonton waved the police boat over. He started to wrap a towel around the wound, trying not to jostle the arrow, but the spear tip had fallen off with all the activity.

Alex hunched reflexively with the pain, and the metal shaft fell out of his arm and clanked against the floorboards. A heavy spurt of bright red blood shot from the wound and spattered Wonton across the chest.

"Christ! Oh shit!" The big man clamped his hand around Alex's arm above the wound. "It's an artery! I need a tourniquet!" He rolled his huge fingers around the biceps and probed until he pressed the torn artery against the bone. He hadn't really believed them in first-aid class—all that stuff about a severed artery being able to shoot blood across the room. And he wasn't about to believe the rest, either—about the two or three minutes it took to bleed to death.

The coast guard captain was on the radio: "Get that chopper back!" he ordered.

Alex felt a huge wave roll through his head and tried to hold it back. "Where's Chicago?" He coughed.

"She's here, she's okay."

Alex turned his head and reached out a hand in her direction. Then he felt a bump as another boat came alongside, heard a new commotion of voices and bodies. Everything was getting wobbly and he tried hard to hold on to consciousness. He saw faces but couldn't make them out. He felt his equipment being unbuckled. Someone slipped a band around his arm and twisted it tight, freeing Wonton.

"She's bent . . ." he forced his voice as loud as he could.

He heard voices and commotion: "I need an IV . . . get the basket over here . . ." A radio crackled.

"She's okay." Wonton was talking right in his ear. "She's all right. You're both gonna be fine."

Alex shook his head. For the first time in this whole stupid escapade, real fear seized him. It was the worst fear—helplessness. He couldn't *do* anything now. He couldn't fix the deadly bubbles that were forming in Chicago's blood. He couldn't grab on to anything. Alex had been shot before, knifed a couple of times, beaten up, and dropped from heights. Each time upon finding himself alive, he knew that he could pull himself together. But here was a simple, clean cut and he couldn't get so much as a handful of himself to restore.

"She's bent," he gasped again. Could Wonton even hear him? "Too deep."

Then he felt the damp weight of Chicago's hair on his chest and her hand on his shoulder.

"Hey," Chicago broke in. "I'm fine. You're funny as bait."

"His pressure's dropping . . . get the Mast suit."

"Shit almighty!" Wonton growled. "Baby, you all right?" He draped one hand on Chicago and looked her over quickly "That's that diving thing—the bends? You got it?"

Chicago shrugged and tried to smile. "Well, probably—yeah."

"Well, what do we do?" Wonton asked her gently.

Alex looked at Chicago and tried to focus. Half her face was scraped and bruised, the blood just starting to dry in dark patches. Strands of hair stuck to the blood, and Alex reached instinctively to brush them away, but his good arm was being tied to the IV board. He squeezed his eyes shut and tried to stay out of the gulf that was washing up around him.

"Hey, she's got the bends. What do you do for that?" Wonton shouted at the coast guard captain. The helicopter basket was being lowered, and two men zipped Alex into the antishock Mast trousers.

"Got to get her to a recompression chamber. We'll take her

along." He shouted orders over his shoulder, and someone got on the radio to call the chamber.

"Meanwhile, give her three aspirin and get her on oxygen and lie her down."

Another stretcher and an oxygen tank were handed up from below. Chicago was fighting back tears, her shoulders trembling. She shook her head. "I'm staying with you," she insisted stubbornly.

"Whoa—getting possessive, are we?" Alex teased weakly. "Hospital's boring. Besides, recompression might . . . do you some good." His breathing was labored, but talk was suddenly his only connection. "Look what it does . . . for Michael Jackson . . ." He tried to lift his head.

Chicago felt hands on her shoulders gently lifting her back.

"So let's . . . get together later on . . . compare notes." His voice was failing.

Chapter 33

Wonton and Umbi paused just inside the room. It was a loud, harsh place, full of clanking and hissing. It was like a space-age boiler room with a collection of knobs, wheels, and gauges. The recompression chamber, an iron cylinder ten feet long and about eight feet high, lay like a toppled garbage can against the far wall. In front of this chamber, a doctor and an engineer stood before a bank of knobs and gauges and valves with the controlled tension of professionals at work.

Over one speaker they heard a crackling voice. "Jesus! Enough already with the pins! What is this, Voodoo 101?"

"Oh yes, mon." Umbi grinned. "Sound like she doin' okay now!"

Inside the recompression chamber, Oscar, the tender, was laughing as he continued to prick Chicago on the feet and legs. He was glad to hear her abuse. She had been a little too quiet when they first brought her in. They got her in fast and she had had only mild symptoms—slight numbness in the extremities, some joint pain, and a real bad temper. No paralysis, no stroke.

"We've cured everything but your language." He laughed as he adjusted the oxygen.

"So are we there yet?" she prodded, brushing sweaty hair off her forehead. She was starting to relax. She felt almost giddy with relief to think that it would soon be over. It was an awful place, this metal tank with its clanking and whooshing noises and hard, hard walls. The inside was bare metal, all industrial gray, with only a thin mat on a metal cot for the patient and a stool for the chamber tender. The atmosphere, pressurized and rich with oxygen, was highly flammable. Flammable, hell. One spark and the place would explode.

The ride "down," as the chamber was pressurized to a simulated depth of 150 feet, was cold and clammy; the ride up, hot and humid. It smelled bad the whole time, like a very antiseptic drain pipe. She felt claustrophobic.

Oscar was short and stocky as a good pair of boots, with a soft disposition and a reassuring presence. He had been a commercial diver for years. He still looked like he could rip bolts off oil rigs with his bare hands, but there was something clucky and calm about him, too. Meeting him on the street, you wouldn't be able to decide if he ran a junkyard or a beauty salon. He made you feel he could fix things: vacuum cleaners, china figurines, broken hydroelectric dams, sick birds. And right here he often had. The chamber had saved many a diver from decompression sickness or, as it was more commonly and dramatically known, the bends.

Although oxygen is—to us, anyway—the important part of air, 80 percent of the air is actually made up of nitrogen. When you breathe compressed air underwater, the nitrogen is absorbed by the body's tissues. All this nitrogen doesn't hurt you; it's an inert gas. It just sort of fills up the space around the oxygen. On a normal, safe dive, following the depth and time limitations of the tables, the nitrogen escapes naturally during breathing and never forms bubbles. Stay too deep for too long or ascend too fast, though, and the nitrogen comes out of solution too fast, and bubbles form in the blood. Suddenly, the body is like a bottle of soda, shaken up and ready to fizz. The bubbles can get lodged in blood vessels, causing paralysis, stroke, or death: the bends.

"Just a little while more, lovey." Oscar smiled as he filled out more charts.

"Lovey, darling, what is this with the cutesies? What do you call some three-hundred-pound hairy-chested marine in here?"

"Anything he wants!" He laughed. Oscar liked Chicago. Too often his patients were assholes—hotshot divers who ignored the tables and stayed too long, pushed the limits as if tempting physiology were an especially brave deed. Then they got bent and scared, and he had to get in the tank with them for six or more hours while they gradually got better and began to fuss and complain, threatening to sue their instructor or the dive-boat operator or Jacques Cousteau for inventing the damn equipment in the first place.

"We're at fifteen feet, darlin'—heading up. I'm calling out for pizza. What do you like on it?"

"Shark," she replied promptly, and they both laughed. Oscar read out her last set of vital signs to the doctor, who recorded them on the chart.

"You've got visitors," the doctor announced and waved Wonton over to the little window. Chicago saw him and leapt to the glass.

"Hey, mermaid." Wonton smiled.

"How's Alex?" She was far from the microphone and her voice sounded tinny and faint.

"He's good. He's out of surgery. They patched the leak and filled him up. He was a couple of quarts low, but he's doing fine."

Umbi squeezed in next to him and grinned. "I give blood." He stepped back away so she could see the bandage on his arm. "Maybe he start turnin' a little dark next few days."

"Oh God. Your blood's likely to sour a snake!"

"Relax," Wonton broke in. "They didn't really use any; they sold it to a witch doctor down the street." He pressed his face closer and tried to see inside the chamber. "Cozy place. My mother used to have one of these. Made a hell of a pot roast."

"Hey, ain't dis some kinda weird karma," Umbi teased. "You the one windin' up in the aquarium now!"

"Shit, I hope not. If this is how it is for the fish, I'll turn in my collecting license right now."

They talked for a few more minutes, but once Wonton knew she was all right, he grew restless. There was too much else to tie up right now. He left cab fare with Umbi, phone numbers with the chamber staff, and made his exit. It was nearly four. Rush-hour traffic would be starting soon; weekend traffic, too. He hurried to his car. His sense of relief over Alex and Chicago was still strong, but it was rapidly fading out under a slow, burning anger.

Torrance was at his desk looking over the arrest reports. He looked up as Wonton came in.

"Frank, I didn't expect you back. Is the girl all right?"

"Yeah, they're almost done with her. She should be okay."

"Good, that's good. I just talked to the hospital. Alex is awake; wants to talk to you. I told them there was no hurry." Torrance smiled. It was a quick smile, a rectangular smile that always looked like an afterthought.

"You two pulled off quite the dramatics," he continued. "The press have been swarming like your shark pack. Good work, though, very good work. We were lucky, too. Heroics never hurt. And a chance like this—Kalispel right into our hands. Well, it's the kind of thing we can usually only dream about."

Wonton looked at the captain closely. It wasn't like him to ramble. There was something oddly tranquil about him, as if he had taken up Buddhism or Thorazine that afternoon.

"So Kalispel's still here?" There was a twinge of sarcasm in Wonton's voice.

"Of course."

"Still alive?"

Torrance looked at him puzzled, pressed his fingers together, and kept a steady gaze. "Of course."

"Is that because Selby's out of the picture now or because you just need a little time to arrange things?"

"What are you talking about?" Torrance responded placidly.

"I'm not all sure yet, but you're about to fill in the blanks. Start with Morales."

"The Morales shooting is still . . ."

Wonton interrupted, "Then go on to the four drug dealers turned loose over the past few years on Judge Selby's orders who were later shot with my old service revolver." He searched Torrance's face for some response. He wasn't sure what he expected to see; he wasn't exactly sure what he had expected to find out.

"What are you talking about?"

"You tell me. No one knows I even have that old thing, let alone where I keep it. What's going on?"

"Wonton . . ." Torrance felt his hands grow cold, a shadow dropped in the room, and he looked out the window to see that the sun had just creased the edge of the office tower across the street. "I'm not sure what you're getting all excited about. You were aware of . . . business."

"Your business stinks." He slapped the desk and turned away.

"Odors aside, there's no big revelation going on. You've been contentedly 'not seeing.' " He paused, searching for the right words, uncomfortable, slightly offended, by calling it a business, as if it were insider trading or some other really despicable crime. ". . . not seeing certain . . . activities for years."

"I'm not talking about the payoffs and bribes. The shit I'm 'not seeing' was supposed to be small stuff—not felony shit, not drug shit, and damn well not murder!" But even as he argued, he felt a growing sense of disgust.

"Are you going purist on me, Frank?"

"There's a difference between fixing tickets and knocking off suspects!" Wonton pointed out, but the edge was off his rage now. What the hell difference did it make really? he thought bitterly. So what if he never took a "real" bribe? He had surrendered his integrity. He had accepted the judge's offer to care for his son, had lied to Ellen all these years, telling her it was a police-benevo-lent-fund program that allowed them to keep Joseph at St. Jude's.

"I don't know what you're talking about," Torrance replied coolly.

"Can the shit. I'm not wired. And if your office is bugged, you'd better turn it off 'cause you're going to talk, and you're going to tell me everything."

"I've done nothing wrong."

"How do you see that?"

The captain answered in a steady voice: "I see it quite clearly. I've done nothing wrong, though it's true, others may not see it that way. But at any rate, there's nothing to implicate you. You didn't do anything. You're out of it."

"Out of it, my ass! People are dead off my gun, I'm set up for an ambush, and your twits are stealing cocaine from my bust and I'm just out of it?"

Wonton walked to the door, glancing out into the station. I didn't do anything, he thought to himself. That's right. I just didn't do anything. It was so easy just to accept it—take care of the kid, just ignore the rest. But there must have been some other way. But hadn't they thought it through hundreds of times?

Joey couldn't stay at home any longer. He had never learned to communicate. He was violent and uncontrollable, banging his head constantly and thrashing out at them. He had terrible seizures. When Ellen became pregnant again, she couldn't handle him. He was strong for a seven-year-old and he hurt her badly once. Few institutions would take such a child and the ones that would were horrible places.

"Wonton, look. We truly had no idea about Kalispel. It took us all by surprise. And I didn't know anything about the missing drugs. Where did you get that from?"

"What do you know about Barnes?"

Torrance shrugged. "It's crossed my mind that she might be on the take, but if she is, she's quiet, she's solo, and it's never caused a ripple. How does she fit it?"

"She knew Kalispel was on his way out to Osprey Reef and she didn't warn us. She may even have tipped him off. She probably stole the coke from the fish market bust."

"So where did all this new suspicion come from?"

"Alex sprang it on me this morning when Kalispel showed up. He thought I was crossing him."

"Sanders?" The captain looked out the window with an air of disinterest, distraction, possibly relief. "He's a fed?"

"I really don't know. We didn't get much chance to discuss it."

Torrance just nodded and continued to stare off into space. "I was starting to wonder about him. We knew there had to be something going on lately."

"He's been investigating Judge Selby, corrupt cops, you, the whole thing."

"Really. So what is the whole thing?"

Wonton continued evenly. "I don't know. How about you and Selby solicit bribes from suspects, you take their money, let them go, and then kill them." And even as he said it, he knew it was true; and even as he knew the truth of it, he couldn't shape an ending. Here they were sitting calmly on a Friday afternoon and the world had to change somehow by the time they left. Wonton hadn't had time for a shower and his skin itched from the saltwater.

"What was the alternative?" Torrance swiveled around in his chair and looked at Wonton calmly. "You know the facts—the courts, the damn lawyers. You know how many we catch who never lose a night's sleep in worry. I did the right thing. I did the noble thing."

Wonton felt like layers of paint were starting to crack and flake off a canvas. A familiar painting that had hung innocuously over the sofa for many years, a painting of a deer family by a forest stream or something, was now showing, in streaks and lines, some terror world by Dali, tilted and awful.

"But you took their money!"

"Selby did. I never spent it. It's all safe."

"So that makes it right?"

"That makes it irrelevant. I took the money because that's how these things are done. I could hardly just say I was letting them go out of the goodness of my heart. It had to be done. And I took the money out of circulation. I diverted it from criminal enterprise."

"What about Selby?"

"He was a toad, greedy. The man had no conscience."

"So you killed him."

"He killed himself. He died of sloth—one of the seven deadly sins."

"Damnit, Alton! When were you canonized?"

Torrance wondered what showed—the weakness at the back of his knees? The tic he felt just under the edge of his right eyebrow? Mostly, he found himself remarkably calm.

"So what now?" he asked flatly.

"What the hell now? I'm a cop. You're a suspect in a murder. You tell me."

The captain nodded. What do I have to arrange, he thought to himself—mortgage, insurance, the children's tuition payments? I have to look over those estimates for the new roof, write down some sort of maintenance schedule for things—oil changes and tire rotations for the car; filter cleanings for the AC. Emma doesn't think of things like that.

"Could you give me some time? I need to take care of some things for Emma, and I'd like to avoid the Sunday papers."

Wonton thought about it for a minute, then nodded. There was little chance Torrance would go anywhere. He was actually glad for the delay—relieved for the moment, anyway.

"Yeah, sure. I'll talk to Alex."

"I could come in Sunday afternoon when it's quiet," the captain offered helpfully.

Chapter 34

But Alton Torrance did make the Sunday papers—the early edition, even—with uncanny precision, allowing just enough time for the first photos to be developed and a quick few paragraphs lamenting the tragedy to be put together. Details would follow in the second edition, along with less grisly photos. By then the editor-in-chief had been called, and he angrily reprimanded the photo editor.

"Shit! People are going to see this over breakfast!"

By the final edition, the one the late risers propped up against napkin dispensers on breakfast counters and uptown yuppies enjoyed over their second cup of fresh-ground french roast, the story had already begun to be fleshed out after the first sensational details.

"Sources say that an FBI undercover operation was about to expose the veteran police captain . . ."

"A letter discovered on the captain's desk revealed . . ."

Wonton was awakened to an automatic and heart-stalling alertness at 3 A.M. by the ringing telephone. He hurried to the hospital and tried to do some damage control on the story.

Rachel had come home late from a date and was still awake, watching the 4 A.M. creature feature (and marveling at the similarities) when she was called with the news. She felt a mixture of deflation and relief. It was her first big, important case; she had done a lot of work and would have liked to see it through to the end. Still, it would be nice to get back to Washington. Summer was over and the fall would be nice. There was a good-looking lobbyist she had gone out with a few times, and maybe now that she had done well on an undercover, she would find her career on a more interesting swing.

Alex didn't find out until 8 A.M. He had been hanging around the nursing station, bugging them to arrange his discharge that day, when one of the morning nurses came in and tossed the paper onto the desk. He saw the headlines and the picture. It was the first edition. He had to sit down. The nursing supervisor got him in a wheelchair and hauled him back to his room, pointing out that this proved it—he was still too weak to be out of bed.

Wonton showed up around nine, looking tired and grim. He pushed Alex's discharge through with remarkable ease, and only explained once they were in the car that a Lieutenant Braddock had called from the FBI requesting that Alex be held in protective custody until the rest of the suspects were brought in. Detective Melissa Barnes, it seemed, could not be located.

Alex spent a surreal day lying on Wonton's living room couch with Kung Fu movies and the dregs of between-season sports on the tube, playing endless games of Candyland with Dusty and trying to piece it all together with Wonton.

It was not until a few days later, when the whole unbelievable story was starting to come out, when the captain began to live again in heated arguments all over the city, that the best headline appeared. HERO OR VILLIAN? There was a special 900 number that readers could call to voice their opinion.

Chapter 35

Alex slipped the last few papers into the box on his desk and glanced around the office to see if he had forgotten anything. There hadn't been much to forget. There were no pictures, no funny coffee mug, no matching desk set and paper-clip box. It's like I've never really been here, he thought. The rubber plant looked a little better, but it wouldn't miss him—his coffee, maybe, but not his care. His injured arm still in a sling, he tried to slide the box off the edge of the desk.

"Oh, Detective Sanders sir, let me help you." The concerned voice of Mrs. James Beaufort startled him as she hurried to his side. "I didn't know you were coming back. I thought—well, I suppose I thought they would just whisk you away in the dead of night."

"No, it's all pretty ordinary. I punch my time card and catch the next train. I just had a few things to pick up."

Mrs. James Beaufort pushed his box back on the empty desk with a half-reprimanding, half-reassuring gesture. "Let me get someone to carry this down for you."

"That's okay, it isn't heavy."

She patted his arm as if reading his thoughts. "Nobody feels harshly toward you. They know . . . well, it wasn't you who did it. You just found it out. You just did your job." Alex nodded

grimly. "Alton Torrance was not a bad man. That makes it difficult. He was respected, but—well, he couldn't go on . . . doing
those things." It came out in a whisper as she automatically
glanced around.

"I know."

"And the others—well, they were purely dishonest. I must say
I was shocked. That nice Melissa. I remember when she first came
on the force. I never suspected. Should I have? I always did think
she dressed a little too rich for a police salary, but you know, you
can often find very nice clothes, designer clothes, in some of the
consignment shops in West Palm Beach. But should I have suspected anything?" The question was in earnest, and Alex felt a
stab of compassion for the elderly woman.

"No, of course not." He squeezed her hand. It was tiny and
soft.

She looked down for a minute, then glanced up at Alex, her
brow was knitted. "Alex, may I call you that?"

"Yes, yes of course," he responded, with an odd fear that she
might be about to reveal her own first name.

"Alex, I have a confession of my own. I don't know what you
have to do about it. I should have come forward when first I
learned of your investigation, but I was afraid. I thought about it
and I decided, though, that I have to tell the truth."

Alex wanted to cringe. What could she be about to tell him?
That she ran a money laundering operation out of her spare
bedroom?

"I'm seventy-three years old," she whispered. She looked down
in shame. "I'm supposed to be retired years ago. I'm afraid I'm
another one of Captain Torrance's . . . arrangements. He kept
me on." She looked up at Alex sadly. "I always hated sitting
home. And I never could stand the thought of doing some old-
lady charity work," she whispered guiltily. "I'm not religious, I

can't knit, and I don't like rocking those little sick babies in the hospital. I like working here. I'm part of his dirty dealing."

Alex felt some bubble rising to the surface like a fumarole, like the sour ferment had finally worked its way up and now threatened to erupt in laughter or tears or punching walls. He swallowed the feeling with difficulty and hugged the old lady.

"Dear Mrs. James Beaufort, you stay right here. That's not a crime. I promise. It's been hard to figure out just what is and isn't a crime in this mess, but I guarantee that's not a crime."

Chicago was sitting in the cab of her truck with her legs stretched out and her feet on the steering wheel, flipping through *Undersea Journal.* She climbed out as Alex approached and took the box from him. He kissed her across the obstacle.

"Where to now?" she asked as she dropped the box in the back of the truck.

"I don't know—Buffalo, Wichita Falls . . . Detroit maybe." He caught her and pinned her against the cab, only slightly stymied by the bad arm. Alex kissed her again, wanting nothing by the scent and feel of her here in the shade. He felt the cool giddiness of escape, like the last day of school or haying, like bad company finally snapping shut their suitcases.

"When's your flight?"

"Tomorrow. Noon. Twenty-four hours. So let's start."

Chicago laughed. "Start what? You don't look like you're ready to do any pushups for a while," she whispered seductively.

"I was kind of thinking of running a halyard through the forward hatch. You know, you could sort of winch me up . . ."

Chicago collapsed in giggles at the thought. Alex kissed the side of her neck. "But then again," he whispered in her ear, "you could always . . ." and he began to describe more fully his suggestions for lovemaking with a wounded arm.

They heard a car approach. Alex reluctantly unclinched and turned half around to see Wonton driving up in the old Impala.

"Hey, when did you get all lovey-dovey? What happened to the rude, insulting, antagonistic people I knew and loved?"

"We were just starting when you showed up."

"Oh well, don't let me interrupt. I'm on my way to the airport. They picked up Barnes in Puerto Rico, ticket in hand to Guadeloupe. She was probably on her way to Paris. You should have seen her place. The lady liked fine things. She's evidently been a regular bidder at Sotheby's."

"Is that why you're picking her up in this piece of garbage?"

"You know, I'm glad you brought that up. I was meaning to talk to you about the damage you caused to this fine automobile."

"Damage I caused?" Alex laughed incredulously as he looked at the battered old car.

"Yeah, look there—paint's scratched, wiper's still broken, and there's one big dent in the shape of your head over the right fender. I mean, after all, it was you who caused it . . ."

"Don't they have some kind of program now," Alex said to Chicago, "where they sink old junked cars to make artificial reefs? Didn't I hear about that someplace?"

"Yeah, they take them out on barges and sink them."

"Oh well, we could always just drive it off the end of the pier."

"You'd need a lot of weight inside to keep it sunk."

"That's true." Alex leaned against the door and poked his head in the driver's window. "How much you weigh, Wonton?"

"Hey, more than a shark at least!" Wonton pointed out as he shifted to forward and lurched Alex off balance. "Lucky for you!" he shouted as he drove off. Chicago and Alex got into the truck.

"So how long will you be in Washington?" She finally broached the subject.

"I shouldn't need more than a couple of weeks or so. Then I'll be back here through the trials."

"How long will that take?"

"Years, if I'm lucky."

"What a line." She sniffed the air in an exaggerated way. "Yeah, horseshit."

As they walked down the dock toward the *Tassia Far,* Chicago and Alex could smell something cooking. Umbi was on deck with the grill fired up, a six-pack of Pilsner Urquel beer on ice, and a disappointed look on his face.

"Hey, my friends. You early—you mess up my surprise!"

"Umbi, what a spread. Looks like we're just in time," Chicago declared as she looked over the feast he had assembled.

"No, mon, I mean to have it all romantic-ready and be gone, in case you want to go below and, like, eat it out of your belly buttons or something in a frenzy of passionate desire thing."

"Umbi, how could we celebrate without your sorry carcass around?" Chicago chided.

"Anyway, I've had enough of frenzies of any sort for the time, thank you very much," Alex said as he stuck his finger into the barbecue sauce for a taste. "Wow! Why don't you just cut our tongues out with a machete!"

"Shut up and have a beer, wimp." Chicago tossed him one and handed another to Umbi. They sprawled around the cockpit enjoying the barbecue. The sky turned a dusty pink, then a deep twilight blue. Umbi slipped away.

Deep in the sea, the night world was blossoming. The brightly colored reef fish were tucked in their nooks for the night while others emerged from hiding to feed. Crabs scuttled fearlessly, octopuses crept from their craggy homes, and moray eels swam free in elegant motion.

There are stars underwater. At night, in this most perfect

world, tiny planktons glow with a luminescence. Suspended like stars, then swirled by motion, the sea is a galaxy of its own.

Deep in the sea, sharks are swimming their eternal rhythms, their perfect shark bodies pure and unchanged for eons. Underwater, everything is right, everything makes sense. There is no malice. The sharks are simply swimming and drawing in their wake glittering star trails.